W9-CGR-043

More reviews for *In The Heart of Things*:

"To his credit, Mr. Lliteras. . .experiments with literary structure, using a Pinteresque play-within-a-play and poetry to reflect his character's metaphysical struggle and awareness."
Ann G. Sjoerdsma
The Baltimore Sun

"*In The Heart of Things* is a worthy novel about two homeless veterans."
Marc Leepson, Arts Editor
Veteran Magazine

"D. S. Lliteras' *In The Heart of Things* is a daring and ambitious book, mixing as it does prose fiction, script, haiku, and renga to show Llewellen's spiritual journey and renewal."
Wayne Ude,
Ghent Magazine

National and international praise for *In A Warrior's Romance*:

"You don't read this book. With a slight touch of embarrassment you look over Lliteras's shoulder and gently finger the old photograph on one side of the page and then linger over his thoughts that are printed on the other side. . . .This is a very fine book, as much for what it doesn't do as for what it does. Few books that make it to the book counter are so devoid of pretension and bombast, especially when it comes to all the first hand accounts about Vietnam."
Robert S. Need
Vietnam Magazine

"Since culture is not fixed, but is always in a state of 'becoming,' those doing the writing inevitably test its limits and shape the form. It was probably inevitable in the ongoing history of western haiku that a writer would come along and make a major adjustment in that shaping by publishing his haiku of war—200 pages worth, in fact. And Lliteras has approached his work with such honesty and mastery of the craft that the haiku community is accepting 'Romance' with open arms as well as open minds."
Mary Lou Bittle-DeLapa
Ko Journal, Nagoya, Japan

"His words are powerful, yet simply stated."
Tom Bartlett, Managing Editor
Leatherneck Magazine

"This book of haiku and photography is a romance about the compassionate warrior. It transcends culture, religion, time, place, and the self. It is one man's look into the heart of his wartime experience in Vietnam."
Dyan Eagles, President
Dharmacraft Catalog

Into The Ashes

A NOVEL

D. S. Lliteras

Jack,

My best wishes

to you.

Danny

10/26/93

HAMPTONROADS
PUBLISHING COMPANY, INC.

Front cover: watercolor by Bessie Cook (1885-1980)
Doncaster, Nottinghamshire, England

Publication Acknowledgements:
"Blends of pink and grey" — Haiku Headlines (CA) 1990
"visible" — Backyard Bamboo (MI) 1990
"open highway. . ." — Mirrors (CA) 1993

For information write:

Hampton Roads Publishing Company, Inc.
891 Norfolk Square
Norfolk, VA 23502

Or call: (804)459-2453
(FAX: (804)455-8907

If you are unable to order this book from your local bookseller, you may order directly from the publisher. Quantity discounts for organizations are available. Call 1-800-766-8009, toll-free.

ISBN 1-878901-77-X

Printed on acid-free paper in the United States of America

*Always dedicated to my loving
wife Kathleen Touchstone. . .*

*and dedicated to my dearest
colleagues and friends:
Frank DeMarco and Bob Friedman*

Preface

Into the Ashes is the second book of a trilogy that begins with *Into the Heart of Things.* The third book of the trilogy, *Half Hidden by Twilight,* is scheduled for publication in 1994.

Although the sequential reading of any trilogy will enrich the reader's experience, it should not be a requirement. Therefore, I have written these three novels in such a manner that they can be read independently. However, those who choose to read the entire trilogy in sequence will discover that these novels are held together by the vision and the quest of a single character; and they will experience the added depth and scope which, by nature, accompany any trilogy.

Contents

In the Heart of Things

Unless we seek beyond our soul
we cannot be the poet,
the day-laborer
that is in us all.

Our rhythm should be of life
in the very presence of things
in the very action of change
in the heart of things:
beyond the knowledge of existence
beyond the time of timelessness:
that eternal universe
not to be feared as in the way we fear
our lives.

Prologue
Ground Zero

My travels back through the past into regions which intersected friends and family members associated with ordinary life had nullified, to some extent, the level of peace that I had obtained through Jansen and company in Baltimore, Maryland. Not that I had achieved any degree of attainment, for as we know, no such level of hierarchy exists when we refer to enlightenment. Yet, we must point to some kind of goal when we use words to describe a quest which denies the use of words.

I had spent several weeks at home. And after recovering from the shock of my physical condition, my parents had showered me with luxuries that softened my will, bringing me to a mental state of imbalance. My inner self was dissipating. I felt alienated once again. And with the hedonistic acceptance of my parents' roast beef, ice cream, and warm bed, this inner self was becoming cluttered with the illusion of enlightenment and the delusion of reality which tormented the reverse side of my empty soul. The more I tried to maintain the steadiness of Baltimore, the more I encountered change.

It was already late in April and brutally hot in Miami, especially after I had just spent an equally brutal cold winter in Baltimore. I sat up on my bed wheezing and blew my nose at what remained of my cold. Florida weather had never agreed with me and I was rather sickly as a child growing up here. I always felt claustrophobic in this humidity and always felt tired from my asthmatic breathing. In fact, this climate seemed to break down my entire immune system and no amount of air conditioning was effective against it. If it weren't for my parents, I would never see Miami, or any place in Florida for that matter, again.

I knew the house was empty. It was eleven o'clock on a

Wednesday morning and my parents had left for work hours ago. I didn't bother to change out of my cotton khaki shorts and white tee shirt. I climbed up the six steps leading from the downstairs bedroom, into the kitchen that was part of the main house at that level. The kitchen was large, painted white, and bright with jalousie windows which extended the entire length of the eastern wall.

I opened the refrigerator out of habit and decided to take out the milk and butter. I placed them both on the round dining table at the center of the kitchen on my way to the stove, where I lifted the kettle to see if there was any water in it to boil. My activity was as methodical as it was mechanical and with the conclusion of my kitchen activity, I found myself seated at the table in front of a cup of coffee with cream and sugar and a hard roll with chunks of butter embedded in the torn half that I was about to eat. But something stopped me. I leaned back into my chair and stared at the coffee, the bread, the crumbs on the table. I released a long, soft sigh.

"You're right back where you started, Llewellen. Ground zero. Here. Home. Nowhere."

I got up from the table and began a tour of the house as if for the first time in my life. Of course, the tour was unnecessary because I grew up in this house and knew every crack and crevice down to its foundation. But the ghost within myself compelled me to go on with my circular search that first led into the Florida room, the most comfortable room in the house.

The cushions to the bamboo furniture were decorated with a tropical floral print upon a dark yellow background. The carpet was deep green, the wood paneling a resinous brown, and the ceiling an antique white. Various still-life paintings tastefully dotted the walls except for the length of the east side wall. Like in the kitchen, a set of jalousie windows ran the length of that wall to a jalousie back door which hung to the extreme right corner of the room; these jalousies permitted the sun to flood the room with daylight. There was just enough height below the jalousie windows for an air conditioning unit to poke through the wall; a large color television stood just to the left of that unit.

The furniture was arranged in the following manner as one turned counterclockwise. Toward the north side of the room stood a couch with a side table; a door leading into a hallway hung in the far left corner. Two easy chairs with a small table between them were placed on the west side of the room facing the windows; two doors leading into the living room hung in the far left and right corners. A cupboard filled with books, family photos, and knick-knacks occupied the south wall and the door leading back into the kitchen formed a rectangular opening in the right corner of that wall.

The Florida room had a way of drawing people into it; actually, capturing its guests. One possible escape was into the kitchen for something to eat. Together, these two rooms formed not only the central nervous system but the heart of this house.

I escaped into the hallway, in spite of my desire to lie down on the couch and waste the rest of another morning staring at the ceiling. I walked into the first bedroom, no longer occupied by my brother or anyone else for that matter, and felt its emptiness: a bed, a bureau, a desk, a closet door slightly ajar. I suppressed the flood of memories that would soon force their way upon me by not coming to a standstill and continued in a slow arc back through the door and into the hallway again. I bypassed the central bathroom without looking in and entered the master bedroom at the end of the hall. After passing through a short alcove with doors leading into walk-in closets on either side, I stopped, spellbound by sensations and observations.

The fragrance of my mother's flowers and perfume invaded the four corners of the room, with the mild scent of mildew from the master bathroom softening its sweetness. A queen-sized bed with a small table on either side, a small wardrobe, a bureau, a wicker chest at the foot of the bed, an upholstered chair with my father's garment rack beside it were traditionally arranged in the rectangular room that was dressed on three sides with large windows covered by Venetian blinds.

I left the bedroom and withdrew down the hall, where I entered the living room through an alternate doorway. Initially, the piano to my right caught my attention as I stood just beyond the doorway's threshold. Thereafter, my study continued in a random manner.

The two handsomely upholstered love seats in front of me were placed face-to-face with a glass-covered coffee table between them; a built-in mock fireplace made of white stone served as their background. Large drapes covering a huge picture window hung on the opposite wall with two upholstered chairs and a table set between them in a configuration similar to that of the Florida room recliners. A large archway with wrought iron trim introducing the dining room took the place of the living room's south wall. The main entrance into the house on the right and an antique tea caddy placed to the left as I faced the dining room provided an additional visual delineation between the two rooms.

A massive walnut dining table with an equally massive storage credenza filled with dishes and a cupboard displaying lead crystal occupied the rectangular space in the only way possible: table at center running the room's length, credenza against the wall on the same side as the picture window in the living room, and the cupboard in the upper left corner of the dining room. Naturally, the door on the left wall led into the kitchen where I started to return. But the thought of eating sickened me, and I went outside through the main door of the house instead.

The humidity struck me immediately as I stepped out into the six-by-six-foot landing which was covered by an aluminum awning. The shade was still good so I sat down at the top of the stairs which led to a paved walkway and squinted uncomfortably toward the outside glare caused by the sun.

Florida heat. It was barely tolerable to me even at this hour of the morning. But I remained outside in an effort to ease my mental discomfort. I leaned back onto my elbows and looked down upon the landing's terra cotta tiles to study a lazy stream of black ants making their way diagonally across the top of the landing; they came up over the edge on one side and went down over the edge on the other side. They appeared and disappeared at such a constant rate that I imagined them to be the same set of ants on a circular treadmill. Such was the state of my mind when an automobile pulled up to the front of the house. I sat up with only a marginal degree of curiosity but I stood up on my bare feet when I recognized who it was getting out of the car.

"French?"

"Llew?"

"It is you."

"I'll be damned."

"How did you know I was back in town?" I asked.

"I didn't," he announced. "I was on my way home when I decided to drive by for old time's sake. I thought I saw you, so I stopped."

French walked across the grass, up the red tiled stairs and sat beside me. We quietly shook hands as we studied each other.

French hadn't changed much. He was heavier, softer, and not quite as blond as he used to be. His amber mustache drooped over both corners of his ever-smiling mouth with a small shock of amber hair growing wildly in the cleft below the middle of his lower lip and above his clean-shaven chin. His pale white complexion highlighted his steel blue eyes, which danced above a round stubby nose tinted red by the sun. His hair grew past his ears on both sides and halfway down his neck in the back; combing it straight back in the front exposed a high forehead. He was about five feet seven inches tall and wore blue jeans and a tee shirt. French released his hand from mine before he spoke.

"I've been worried about you."

My face must have betrayed my silent alarm.

"Your parents told me about Catherine. . .and about your disappearance."

"Oh."

"Are you alright?"

"Who's alright these days?"

French leaned back upon his elbows in a fashion similar to my posture before his arrival.

"Good point," he answered.

"Miami," I said distastefully. "You've never left this damn town, have you?"

"To go where?"

"Anywhere. Away."

"You're back."

"Not for long."

"It's not such a bad town."

"I hate it."

"You always have."

"Have you seen Willie and Tommie?"

"We run into each other from time to time. Tommie is thinking about moving in with me."

"Really?"

"You know Tom; he can't handle money. His finances are a mess. He still actually goes hungry toward the end of each pay period. He makes enough money to get by on but. . .you know Tommie. I'm going to have to be a mother hen for a while."

"Good for you," I remarked with sincerity.

"So. . .what are you doing now?"

"I'm going crazy," I said.

"Seriously. What are you doing with yourself?"

"Nothing." French looked at me as if expecting me to say more. "I mean it."

"Nobody does nothing, Llew."

"That's right."

French decided to change the subject.

"Willie joined the Marine Corps."

"Yeah? So, what's he doing back home?"

"He's AWOL," French flatly said.

"I see. Is Janet still married to him?"

"Yes."

"That's miraculous," I said as I stood up. "Let's go somewhere."

"Sure."

"Come inside while I get dressed."

I didn't know how restless I'd become in the last few days. French's appearance was like a fresh wind whistling around you on a cold day: telling you about the life surrounding you; reminding you of your own delicate mortality as you struggled for the warmth deep within the folds of your winter coat. But that was Baltimore, Maryland, creeping into my presence once again. And this was Miami, Florida, a million years later; a place with its own kind of wind.

Before long, I was dressed in a pair of blue jeans and a tee shirt and was tying off the laces to my sneakers while riding alongside French. The car sped down 62nd Avenue and when French turned right onto Bird Road, he asked me where I wanted to go. I indicated anywhere with a hand gesture. So he kept going straight. The windows were down, the music was up, and I was somewhere in between the past and the present.

I recognized Dixie Highway after we traversed Coral Gables; this was the present. I thought about how many times in my life I had sat in a car waiting for that traffic light to turn green; this was my past. My low-grade anxiety returned.

"Are you all right?" French cautiously inquired.

"Is it that obvious?" I asked.

French didn't answer.

I turned away from him and looked out through the opened side window.

"I've learned nothing, French. I'm right back where I started. Ground zero. Less than zero. Zero means emptiness. Less than zero means I'm still trying to gain something; I'm simply looking at the other side of the same coin."

"I'm not sure I understand what you're saying."

I chuckled for the first time in days.

"Then that makes two of us."

The traffic light turned green and French drove across Dixie Highway.

"Are we going to the Grove?" I asked.

"If that's all right with you."

I melted back into my seat with approval and looked out the window with the restored interest that usually accompanies anticipation.

Yes, I thought. Back where I started. Ground zero. Here. Home. Nowhere.

> daylight
> through a window
> quietly reflecting
> my! the stillness of the outside
> inside

Chapter 1
"You think too much."

Coconut Grove had changed and I had asked French not to stop. He kept driving. We ended up sitting on a cement ledge at the end of a parking lot facing South Beach. The sun bore down upon us but the moderate winds swept away its hot rays.

"I'm trying not to go crazy, French."

French hesitated before he spoke.

"What the hell happened to you in Baltimore?"

"I can't explain that to you. And, I'm not sure anymore."

"So, shut up and don't ask you that question anymore. Is that it?"

"Yeah. Thanks."

We sat quietly together for a long time, until the cessation of the wind forced me to get up and start walking toward the ocean's edge. French followed me without question. The manner of my behavior must have indicated to French that there wasn't any destination since there was no rush of anticipation from him when he caught up with me; he simply positioned himself to my left side and fell in step. We plodded through the wet hard-packed sand, still wearing our shoes, in a zigzag pattern created by the irregular approach of a foaming surf.

"Just because you left home, doesn't mean that everyone who stayed here has remained the same." I stopped walking and addressed French with my eyes. He continued to speak. "Coconut Grove changed because people change. I'm a people."

I digested the inference of my taking him for granted; of my assumption that French was the French I knew from our past.

"Sorry," I said.

"Wasn't looking for an apology."

My gaze into his eyes deepened.

"That's more like it," French said, responding to the change in my countenance.

A cloud, a barrier separating me from the world since Jansen's death, suddenly disintegrated. It was if I had been abruptly awakened in the way Jansen had awakened me so many times before. Was this an accident? A coincidence? By the look in French's eyes, I was sure of it. For one brief moment, the essence of everything Jansen had taught me flashed across my mind. This left me with a single distilled insight, the source of which was a recollection of what Jansen had once said to me, "All sentient beings are enlightened. But only a few are awake."

French was not awake. But he was an intelligent and compassionate human being.

"You think too much," he said.

"I know. That's what someone told me once."

We continued our zigzag progress along the beach within the sound of the surf.

> shadow
> on the sand or
> in the sun around me
> that's making a dark figure from
> behind

Chapter 2
Nuts.

French deposited me at my parents' home with a promise that he would be back that evening. There were probably two solid hours before my parents would be home from work. Plenty of time to pack, write a note, and depart from their existence. I knew I had to go. I was doing them a favor. But parents, loving parents, would never admit to that. And what about a friend? Well, I knew French would understand.

I packed a few items of clothing in a small canvas bag along with a minimum of toiletries. A few cans of food with an opener and a spoon were wrapped in a poncho and a poncho liner; my bedding. It all fit quite nicely into the canvas bag.

As for money, I had thirty-three dollars folded alongside a driver's license in my wallet.

I threw on a long-sleeved shirt and an old wide-brimmed bamboo hat to keep away the sun. I caught the image of myself in the mirror above the chest of drawers. I felt like Vincent van Gogh. I looked as mad.

I walked into my parents' bedroom and entered their walk-in closet. The pleasant odor of cedar mixed with the human smell of clothes caressed my olfactory senses and catapulted me into an emotional episode: it was possible that I would never see them again. I hoped they knew I loved them.

I toyed with the idea of waiting for them to come home before I left. But an imaginary daydream gently unrolled before me with an accurate vocal ring that sounded like a play:

Mom:	What are you doing to yourself?
Llewellen:	I don't have a self.
Pop:	You talk crazy.
Llewellen:	Everything would be simple if that were true.

Pop:	(Disgusted) You're throwing your life away.
Llewellen:	So that I can find it.
Pop:	(Looking at Llewellen's mother.) See?
Mom:	(As if Llewellen weren't present.) No, Jack. He's a good son.
Pop:	Who said he wasn't? Nuts.

I located my father's fountain pen and writing tablet, which was the purpose of my visit into their closet, and wrote:

> Dear Mom and Pop,
> Forgive me. I know you
> will. Had to escape. I'll
> call.
>
> Love,
> LL

Chapter 3
It's all a dream.

I gasped for air as I sat up from my supine position in response to the vividness of my dream. It shattered my slumber and I found myself panting into the wind and the surf. I had slept on a beach that night. First time. I felt like hell. Sand had managed to find every moist fissure in my body.

After realizing that I felt too tired to stand up, I leaned back with both my hands behind me and reached for what was left of my dream. Jansen was alive in what was becoming a string of episodic recollections about him. He was smiling into a Baltimore wind as predictably as I would be frowning into that same wind. His straight dark hair danced periodically in response to an occasional gust. But he did not appear disheveled. And he was not wearing his old Navy surplus peacoat; I always had a difficult time visualizing him divested of this distinctive garment. He appeared naked without it. His lean frame resembled a stuffed scarecrow: fragile under a uniform comprised of a thin sweater and an old pair of blue jeans.

I rolled over onto my stomach and almost pressed my face down into the sand. I began to sob.

I cupped my hands together and buried my eyes from the dawn that was approaching from the Atlantic's horizon. It was not good. My life was still no good. Suddenly, memories of my wife flooded my self-imposed darkness and I began to cry with tears until my nose began to run. I sniffed and coughed and inhaled spasmodically through my mouth. This was enough to agitate the sand that was just an inch or so below these orifices.

I rose to my knees choking on the sand, hating myself even more for my stupidity. I spit out the sand as best I could and approached the water's edge. Then I looked into the brand-new sun.

"Why did Catherine have to die?"

I felt the hopelessness of my question and sank down onto my rump. The surf washed across my shoes and buttocks. I placed my forehead against my knees and listened for my answer.

Jansen's image reappeared with mine alongside him. I was willing to accept anything, even a daydream.

"You and your attachments," he said.

"What are they?" I asked.

"A part of your ignorance," he answered.

"You talk too much."

"I know. I have failed you."

"I can't help myself. I have to cry."

"Then cry."

I looked at him with surprise.

"Nobody said you shouldn't have feelings," Jansen said.

"You make me crazy."

"Crazy, not crazy; satisfied, dissatisfied. Just look with a clear mind! Release yourself. . .from your mental vise."

Jansen rose to his feet.

"Where are you going?" I asked.

"Where I have always been."

"I don't want you to leave."

Jansen grabbed me gently by the throat with both hands. "You still don't get it. I'm not going anywhere." He released his grip. "I have never been anywhere."

"I can't even control my own daydream," I muttered.

"It's all a dream. Stop stringing your words together."

Jansen took a couple of steps back and away from me without releasing me from his steady gaze. He was now wearing his peacoat. His sudden smile accented the angularity of his unshaven face.

"Don't worry," he said. "You're here with me. Among the many. You simply don't know it yet."

I dissolved the daydream by rubbing both of my burning eyes with the palms of my hands. Then I looked up and out into the clarity of the ocean and felt the essence of myself; not Jansen. I had to smile.

"I'm a lunatic." I rose to my feet. "Now. Where do lunatics go from here?"

I shook out the sand from the wadded-up poncho liner I had slept on and stuffed it into my canvas bag. Then I picked up my bamboo hat and screwed it onto my head before slinging the canvas bag over my shoulder. I was a ship without a compass, a watch, or a sextant. Worse than that; I had nothing but the sun and the coast to pilot by in a world where suns and coasts did not exist.

"But there they are!" I shook my head. "Oh where. . .just where was this world going to take me?"

Chapter 4
Intermezzo

I am Robert Llewellen and I am without knowledge. I failed my chemistry final examination.

I just didn't give a damn about my grades. There would be plenty of time to correct the result of this attitude. Besides, the Vietnam War had cut a giant hunk out of my life and I felt like I had already fallen behind my generation. There was no way that I could ever hope to catch up—whatever that meant. Yet, I did feel empowered by the one great gift the war had given me: the rest of my life. So, time was a value without a clear definition. And the battle about its loss or gain raged within me. What did time mean to me? I didn't know. I was getting married today and college chemistry would simply have to wait.

Catherine was staying with her parents two and a half hours away by car; spending the summer thinking about her life—probably numbed by the thoughts of her pending marriage to me—while I was motivated by the GI Bill to continue my studies through the summer months because it was my only source of income.

I loved her. I missed her. And I left Tallahassee to see her at Fort Walton Beach every weekend. My studies may not have gone well that summer quarter but my grade point average in love and romance was a perfect four point oh.

The empowered side of my psyche had won the day. And I was feeling lucky that I had survived the war. One other guy from my unit, who was also my best friend in Vietnam, had survived. His photo album had become an obituary of pictures: eighteen-year-old ghosts, frozen with forever smiles.

Dead. All dead. Killed in action. Nothing could ever be that important again that I would forget the ephemeral gift of life. Fuck chemistry. I'm getting married. I was empowered.

The drive to Fort Walton Beach was pleasant. The hot August

wind blew through the open windows of my car and teased the grey suit I had lying on the back seat. It was the only suit I owned and it was going to be decorated with a single white carnation and a white tie for my wedding.

I was not exhausted by my summer studies and weekend trips to Catherine. I was young and had the strength of the universe within me. I was happy for the first time in my life: I was in love.

Auburn hair, green eyes, fair skin, and a slim five-foot-two figure of less than one hundred pounds comprised Catherine's radiant and sexually attractive outer aspect. Honesty, rationality, generosity, intelligence, and her love for me comprised just a portion of her beautiful inner aspect.

Catherine. What is in a name? Everything.

How could I possible explain who and what this precious human being meant to me? How could I explain something I did not fully understand myself?

I didn't want to understand.

I didn't have to.

I was getting married.

There was no great ceremony upon my arrival, just the most important thing in my life: Catherine's kiss, followed by a hug. Her wedding dress was hanging in her bedroom closet: a short white sleeveless dress with light blue trim around her hemline that came up above her knees. She had been actively waiting for me all day and it felt good to be the recipient of her love and affection.

Several of our friends appeared wearing bathing suits. They had stopped by on their way home from the beach and they were surprised to find out what Catherine and I were doing. A couple of them responded enthusiastically by going to a liquor store and buying beer and cold duck wine. This inspired Catherine's parents to go to a bakery to buy a cake because the one her mom had been baking for us had burned in the oven. The family was beginning to experience the last minute jitters over our wedding, so naturally everything was going wrong.

I was obliviously happy.

Catherine was obliviously in love.

Everybody at the house was excited. I even called my parents and told them I was getting married. They weren't surprised. They knew about Catherine and they knew that I was in love. Catherine had only been a voice on the telephone to them, but they had given her their blessings.

Within an hour, Catherine was in her dress, I was in my suit, more friends had been alerted, and too much cold duck had been drunk; the cake was cut, photographs were taken, kisses shared, and a rolled-up fifty-dollar bill was pressed into my hand in the disguise of a handshake by my future father-in-law before we were poured into my 1959 Ford Fairlane 500.

I backed out of the driveway and aimed the car for Andalusia, Alabama, where Catherine and I got married by a justice of the peace.

*   *   *   *

She scraped the top layer of skin off my finger when she pushed my wedding ring on. She was nervous. We had said, "I do."

We had been pronounced husband and wife in front of two witnesses: a city hall secretary and an elderly lady who had been invited off the street on our behalf. Five dollars had been the ceremony's cost, which included the license and marriage certificate.

It was a marvelous experience and we were happy and young and in love and heading for Pensacola, Florida, for a week-end honeymoon.

> without a conductor
> the mocking birds were singing
> beautifully
> for reasons of their own
> persisting
> here and there and without
> the unnecessary encouragement
> of an encore

Chapter 5
Almost too glad.

"That's not much of a breakfast."

The lady sitting beside me on the cement quay wall which separated the sandy beach from the parking lot startled me. I hadn't noticed her approach. In fact, I was surprised at the close proximity of her presence. I raised my left hand in order to present a better view of the can.

"What's wrong with pork and beans?" I asked.

She was blonde, blue-eyed, too thin, but attractive. She had a Styrofoam cup half filled with black coffee in one hand and a cigarette in the other.

"I don't think a dietician would approve of your morning meal," I added unmaliciously.

"How do you know this isn't the end of my breakfast?" she asked.

"How do you know I'm not eccentric?" I answered.

"Are you?"

"Not yet." I pointed at her cigarette and coffee with my spoon. "So. . .is that breakfast?"

"Yes."

"Then we're having breakfast together," I concluded without triumph.

I plunged my spoon into the lumpy pinkish mass of beans and scooped out a portion. She turned her gaze toward the ocean in response and took a deep drag from her cigarette. She seemed unable to watch me take my next bite. I shoveled the spoonful into my mouth.

We sat together in silence while we finished our breakfast. We allowed ourselves an occasional glance at the other; eye contact was kept to a minimum.

She had a large bruise on her left arm. Her breasts were small.

Her back was straight. Each of these observations had been made at a glance.

I wondered what part of the whole she was seeing of me.

"You're good-looking," she said.

"And you're pretty," I countered.

"I wonder what ugly people say to each other?"

"Only deformed people usually consider themselves ugly," I answered, not knowing where I had derived that conclusion.

"That's a generality."

"So?"

"They're almost always wrong."

"Then I'm no exception."

She fully turned toward me.

"Say, you're okay."

"What does that mean?"

"That I usually don't like people. You're honest."

"I'm not malnourished."

"And you can admit that you may be wrong."

"That's because I don't know anything."

"Then my name is Frances."

"I'm Llewellen."

A short comfortable silence formed a bridge between us again. I looked out toward the beach and traced the short path of footprints I made from the area I had slept to where I was sitting. I had to smile at myself. I hadn't piloted very far down the coast before I discovered I was hungry and settled on top of this cement quay wall facing the Atlantic Ocean. But I was glad. Almost too glad. I suddenly felt uneasy. Frances sensed this immediately.

"What's wrong?" she asked.

"I don't know," I answered.

"Is it sexual?"

"I don't think so."

"Good. Let's not make that a big issue between us. If it happens, it happens; if not, not." She misunderstood my slight attack of indigestion. "Are you married?"

I chucked my spoon into the empty can and set it down between us.

"You're right," I said.

"You're married?"

"No. Beans don't make a good breakfast."

"So far so good."

"You're not afraid to say anything."

"I choose my friends carefully."

"My friends call me Llew."

"Mine call me Fran." She suddenly appeared disappointed. "You don't smoke."

"What's wrong with that?"

"I'm out of cigarettes."

"I've got some money."

"You should keep that kind of information to yourself."

Where had I heard that before? Jansen's image flashed through my memory. This was the second time she startled me.

"Who are you?" I asked.

"You look like you've seen a ghost."

"No. But I'm beginning to believe in karma."

"What's that?"

"You don't want to know."

"But I do want a cigarette."

"Okay. It's on me."

As I rose to my feet, I snagged the spoon out of the empty pork and beans can and stuck it into my mouth to lick it clean. It reminded me that I had a little indigestion. I threw the spoon into my canvas bag and hoisted it over my shoulder. Fran had remained seated. She looked at me uneasily for the first time. I didn't want to ask her what was wrong. I was afraid she was having second thoughts. I decided that was alright, too. So I turned my back to her and looked up into the bright blue sky.

"Damn. This is going to be a beautiful day."

She was standing beside me when I turned back around. She was wearing blue jeans and a tee shirt. Her hair was cut very short; almost boyish. I was momentarily stunned by her fragile beauty.

"You shouldn't smoke," I said.

"I know, it causes cancer."

I stepped off the cement ledge and onto the parking lot. She followed close beside me. She didn't have a purse. I also noticed she had a limp. But it wasn't the crippled, permanent type; I don't know why I knew that. It had been a recent injury; like that bruise on her arm. She allowed me to ignore it. She looked at me with eyes that said this was not the time to explain what these injuries were about. I slowed down my pace. And as I looked away from her, I heard her sigh softly, almost gratefully.

Chapter 6
Intermezzo

Dead. Killed in action.

With a ballpoint pen, my best friend in Vietnam had written the letter D on the figure of every man that had been photographed for his album. D stood for dead and that singular tattoo was marked on all poses—sitting, standing, eating, or laughing; poses which were combined in a variety of pictorial compositions. This was a photo album about ghosts: people who were gone forever, who would not be remembered.

And what about us: me and Sandy? Were we ghosts, too? What had become of us?

Sandy: wounded in action; in and out of Veteran's Hospitals for physical and psychological problems; still and forever wearing a camouflage jacket and a bush cover; still and forever speaking in a bush soldier's jargon that had fallen into the category of archaic English language.

And me: wounded in action; in and out of my self; still and forever a casualty of this world. Was it the war? I'll probably never know. . .in what manner I survived.

> realization: me
> and one other guy left
> from our combat unit;
> the rest were KIA—
> killed in action
>
> the ghosts of laughter; young men
> appearing without the structure of the mind.
>
> realization: too many
> years later, faces

in a photo album, faces
shared with one other, faces
of eighteen-year-olds, forever

* * * *

We had no reservations and it was late in the afternoon when we finally arrived in Pensacola. It never occurred to either one of us that this was August, the season for summer vacationers. But Catherine and I were too innocent to be aware of any of that or to be without luck.

We stopped at the first motel we saw and were unaware that it was a second-rate affair. The owners, an elderly couple, knew who we were immediately and offered us their black and white television from their lobby and an ice chest for us to use for the weekend. It was an unselfish act of kindness on their part; we probably reminded them of who they once were. Anyway, it was their honeymoon gift to a marriage not much older than two hours. The radiance of our smiles and the tenor of our thanks must have been contagious because we left them filled with the spirit of our joy.

The following morning was luxurious to the point of physical decadence: we swam in the motel's unheated swimming pool before breakfast. Life was a dream even though it was only bacon and eggs, toast, grits, and coffee; even though it was an afternoon nap after our lovemaking; even though it was a simple walk on the beach; even though it was improvised laughter over nothing and kisses without any premeditation. All ordinary things and yet, life was fresh and new each moment and, therefore, life was a dream.

radiating with joy:
"it's not me
it was her"
joyful existence
which made whatever
I called the truth,
mine

Chapter 7
Jansen's Thoughts

She was not particular about her cigarettes. She asked for the cheapest brand.

We sat down on round swivel stools covered with blue vinyl, trimmed with stainless steel, and bolted to the floor in front of a long counter. This was a drugstore cafe of the old school, one of the last of its breed, a leftover from another time, another Miami. I bought coffee for both of us.

"Body and mind are not two," I said.

"What was that?" Frances asked.

"I'm sorry," I said. "Just something someone told me once. I was daydreaming."

She lit another cigarette.

"You smoke too much."

"You think too much."

I chuckled.

She looked puzzled.

"Just something someone told me once," I repeated.

The Florida sun attacked us as soon as we left the drugstore. Its bright glare momentarily stopped us at the edge of the sidewalk. I put my hat back on to shield my eyes and squinted for a destination with some shade. But before I could make that location, a car pulled up beside us and honked its horn.

"Where the hell have you been? I've been looking all over for you."

It was French.

"How did you find me?" I asked.

"On foot? How far could you go? Come on, hop in." He looked at Frances. "Who's this?"

"She's with me."

I looked at her to check if this were true.

"We just finished having breakfast," she said to French, with eyes saying yes to me.

I opened the car door and watched her slide toward the middle of the front seat where she would be between French and me. As soon as I slammed the door shut beside me, French handed me an envelope.

"What's this?" I asked.

"It's a letter from Baltimore. It came with your mom and dad's mail yesterday."

"You saw them?"

"I came by to pick you up last night, remember?"

"Sorry."

I looked at my letter.

It had a YMCA return address scribbled on the back of the envelope. I carefully tore it open and found out it was from Zack.

"Who's it from?" French asked.

"A friend," I answered. "Nobody you would know."

French pulled away from the curb and drove down the street. I didn't ask where we were going. And Frances didn't ask what was in the letter. I read.

Dear Llew,

By now words will be of some comfort to you. It is hoped by all of us here (Fish and Largo) that you are no closer toward reaching your goal. Because if you use a goal as a measuring stick, you will get there. And this will simply leave you with the understanding and not the realization that there is no place to go; no place to be.

Remember:

zen takes everything
leaving you nothing:
even as you sit
stop thinking
even as you think
stop sitting
with understanding:
zen gives nothing

Words. Jansen was better at words.

I found a temporary home. It's cheap and, from time to time, Fish and Largo find this place a nice way to escape from the cold or the heat of the streets.

Take care of yourself. You're welcome to write anytime.

Our thoughts are together.
You are not alone.
Zack

I folded the letter back into its original condition and slipped it back into the envelope.

"Where are you taking us, French?"

"To my house. The both of you can stay with me."

"I can't let you do that," I said.

"It's an empty house. You'd be doing me a favor by filling it up."

I looked at Frances but she refused to say anything.

"Thank you," I said. "But you must promise to tell me the minute I've—we've—worn out our welcome."

"I promise to throw you both out that very minute."

Attachments, I thought.

I had been running away from attachments and here I was surrounded by them: a friend, his home, and a woman I was easily growing used to.

But if you are alone and running away, don't cling to that either, I thought.

I smiled to myself. Jansen's thoughts. They always managed to reach out and touch me when I needed them the most. I looked down at my letter.

Zack is Jansen, Jansen is Llewellen, I thought.

I was reading myself; holding a letter that was myself; all of us separate, yet all of us the same. I was confused.

I slumped down on my seat into a relaxed repose and enjoyed all that was happening to me. I looked past a woman I didn't know to a friend who didn't know me and wondered, where was this all leading to now?

I looked out the car window.

> Blends of pink and grey
> colors for a canvas sky. . .
> Where does one begin?

Chapter 8
"If you must know. . ."

The midmorning light barely filtered through the curtains of French's living room. I kicked off my sneakers and felt the coolness of the terrazzo floors penetrate my feet as he turned down the central air conditioning. The house was dark and cool and heavily shaded by the trees outside. French guided us down a hallway and showed us a room.

"You guys can stay here," he said.

I stepped into the room and laid my canvas bag on the floor at the foot of the bed.

"Thanks," I said.

French noticed Frances and me exchange an evasive glance.

"I've only got two bedrooms," French augmented in self-defense.

"Llew did say I was with him," Frances said as she stepped into the room to join me. "You're very kind, French."

"Yeah, well, I guess I'll let you two get settled. I'll be in the kitchen. You guys want any coffee?"

"Sure," I said.

French disappeared without waiting for Frances to respond. She shut the door as if we were married. She smiled.

"French seems like a nice guy," she said.

"He is." A small silence occupied the short distance between us. "I'll sleep on the floor."

"You don't have to do that. We're big boys and girls here."

I did not insist. I liked her. I felt at ease with her. I even liked that I didn't know or care whether this meant anything more than that.

"Do you have any extra clothes?" I asked, knowing it was a stupid question. It would have been easy for her to respond with a sarcastic answer. But I was glad to find out that this kind of attitude was not a part of her nature.

"All I've got is what I have on my back," she answered almost apologetically.

"Don't worry," I said. "We'll figure something out."

"That will be a first time for me."

I chuckled. "You caught me in a lie already," I said. She limped over to the bed and sat down. "You haven't been on the streets very long."

"Since last night. That's long enough." She sighed with reconciliation. "If you must know. . ."

I waved my hand for her to stop whatever she was going to say before I could get my words out.

"You don't have to say anything. I'm nobody. I am not making any judgments."

She placed her hand on the large bruise she had on her upper left arm and studied the injury as if she were assessing the damage.

"He beat me for the last time." She looked up at me. "My boyfriend. My ex-boyfriend. I don't know why I let it go this far. I don't know why I didn't leave him sooner." She looked at the large black bruise. "I left everything behind. I won't go back."

"Then stay," I said, "with me."

She didn't look up. I turned away and walked to the window. I closed my eyes and clenched the window sill.

What the hell was I saying? I thought. I was giving her the impression that there was somewhere to go. That I, me, had something going. I was blowing with the wind! There was no way I could take her along. I didn't have the time or the resources to mend a bird with a broken wing.

She broke into my thoughts.

"Are you alright, Llew?"

I opened my eyes and tilted my head back toward her.

"I think too much, remember?"

She fell back onto the bed.

"Do you mind if I lie down for a little while? It's been a long night for me."

"Sure. Get some rest," I said. Then I pointed to my canvas bag. "You're welcome to anything in my bag."

She closed her eyes before she said thank you to me. I sensed a mood change in her which encouraged me to linger by the door for a moment. I was going to ask her, for the first time, if there was anything wrong until I saw teardrops squeezing past her closed eyelids. I quietly opened the door and guided myself away from her presence. Then I remained motionless in the hallway after I closed the door behind me just in case she wanted to call me back. She didn't.

I turned my attention to my bare feet as they slapped against the cool terrazzo surface on my way to the kitchen. French was already sitting at the kitchen table expecting me.

"What is she all about, Llew?"

"I don't know. Is that instant?"

"Yeah. The jar is right over there. The water is still hot."

I made a cup of coffee and sat at the opposite side of the table. We stared at our coffee instead of each other.

"Are you ever going to get over Catherine?" French queried cautiously.

"What I'm doing has nothing to do with Catherine. I'll always love her. But that part of me is over."

"So, what are you doing?"

"You wouldn't understand."

"Try me."

"I don't understand," I said irritably. "We'll be out of here by tomorrow."

"The both of you can stay here as long as you like. I don't mean to pry, Llew."

"I know. I'm sorry."

"Your parents are worried about you."

I noticed a huge bulk of newspaper bound by a thick rubber band. It had been placed on top of a counter near the refrigerator.

"Is that today's paper?" I asked.

French got up and brought it to the table. "Yeah. Let's break it open."

I stared blankly at the front page while French separated the newspaper looking for the editorial section. He momentarily stopped his search when he noticed my blankness directed toward him. My words were not a reflection of myself when I spoke.

"If you must know. . . ."

French ruffled the section of newspaper he had in his hand in a gesture for me to stop talking.

"Not now, Llew. When you're ready." He looked down at the

first page of the editorial section. "Now, let's see what these predictable idiots have to say. I wonder what bit of freedom they want to take away from me today. I don't know why I bother reading this stuff. It's hopeless. Everyone wants everyone else to pay for their cause. Everyone thinks the other guy is the crook and more governmental control is the answer."

My genuine appreciation for French brought my eyes back into focus.

"Thanks, French."

"For what?"

"For being a friend."

"There's nothing to it."

French hid behind his newspaper in an effort to avoid my gratitude or, worse, my affection. I allowed him to escape and said nothing more. There was no gain and no loss between us. French was being French and I was being myself. It was going to be a Herculean task not to take him for granted. I mustn't. I wouldn't. Tomorrow I would look for a job.

Chapter 9
What is alone?

The house was quiet and I was still seated at the kitchen table. French had gone to his bedroom to take a nap; the search for me had worn him out. A half an hour passed before I rose from the table and made a search through his kitchen cupboard for some paper and a pencil. I discovered a steno pad with a ballpoint pen stuck through its spiral binding. I pulled the pen out and opened the notepad as I returned to my seat at the table. And before I mentally primed myself with thoughtful inquires, I wrote down two words: Dear Zack.

I laid the pen down beside the pad and reached into my pocket for his letter. I read it carefully, then reread it again. I took a deep breath before laying the letter on the table and picking up the pen.

> Dear Zack,
> My zazen has taken a turn for the worse. My posture is poor. My sitting is erratic. I confess Zen gives nothing because I give nothing. Does this mean that I have reached a goal? Because I am nowhere. I know. I'm being stupid.
> Yes, it is a comfort to hear from you. And I thank you for reaching out to me in this manner. I too have found a temporary home and can be reached at the return address on the envelope.
> Say hello to Fish and Largo. My thoughts are with you.
> > What is alone?
> > Llew
> P.S. How did you know where to find me?

I tore the page out of the notepad and prepared it for an envelope by folding it, lengthwise, in half. I returned to the cupboard and searched it again until I found a box of white number ten envelopes. I took one, knowing French wouldn't mind, and deposited my letter into the safety of its enclosure. Then I addressed the envelope, referring to Zack's YMCA address in Baltimore, and added a return address by referring to French's recent telephone bill.

After replacing everything where it had been, I propped the sealed envelope between the salt and pepper shakers and walked into the living room, where I collected three small cushions from the sofa and the easy chair. I stacked them on top of a small throw rug in front of the coffee table and immediately sat upon them without allowing myself that moment of thought which would lead to my inevitable anticipation of pain.

I crossed my legs, then pulled my right leg over my left thigh. I leveled my head, tucked in my chin, straightened my back, placed my left hand into my right palm with my thumbs just touching, and lowered my eyes as I exhaled: what is alone?

> To simply count out
> ten perfect breaths. . .Yes, that's all!
> That's eternity

Chapter 10
Subhuman

I was a statue standing on the threshold of a partially opened door. Fran was still asleep. The sound of her rhythmic breathing accented the silence of the bedroom. I studied her.

She was lying on her side. Her close-cropped blonde hair glowed in the soft sunlight that filtered through the white window shades. Still; very still. Soft; her nature hidden beneath a semi-tough exterior. Gentle; in direct contrast to the harsh world which produced a limp in her gait and a bruise upon her perfection. Such disfigurements, although temporary, were unforgivable. I directed myself away from the brutish result of a former action and momentarily concentrated my thoughts upon the perpetrator: animal. I stopped. I reevaluated my deduction. Then I amended my hasty conclusion after apologizing to the animal kingdom for dragging their purity into the mud.

Subhuman. That's where he belonged: outside the system of man's classification; neither plant nor animal. No Kingdom. No Phylum. No Class. No Order. No Family. No Genus. No Species.

I leaned against the doorjamb satisfied with my conclusion. Satisfied with the non form of life I'd created: non animalia, non chordata, non mammalia, non primate, non hominidae, non homo, non sapiens. Frances stirred in her sleep. I held my breath as she bent her left leg at the knee and crossed it over her right thigh; I exhaled as soon as she was at rest again.

Her facial features were neither too small nor too delicate. In fact, they were perfectly balanced by the moderate fullness of her lips, the gentle curve of her nose, the intricate formation of her ears, and the perfect placement of two sockets; the receptacles for a pair of eyes which I remembered to be the color green.

My eyes shifted down to her figure. Her milky white skin somehow accentuated a natural hairlessness that was quite feminine. She did not need a bra, nor was there an outline of one through her tee shirt. And although she was completely flat-chested, her slim figure was anything but boyish. This curious phenomenon aroused me. But I suppressed that feeling and pressed on with the study of her physical features.

She was about five feet two inches tall and weighed no more than a hundred pounds. Her small hands and slender fingers were in direct harmony with her small bare feet, which displayed ten stubby digits for toes.

She restlessly shifted onto her back. I could sense wakefulness making its approach. I stealthily backed my way through the entrance and pulled the door closed between her presence and mine. I suddenly felt barren standing in the hallway of this strangely quiet house. I walked into the living room knowing that it would be some time before Frances would actually leave the safety of her bed. So I planted myself on French's living room sofa. I noted my fatigue as I lay on my side and equally noted the fringes of my arousal return as I focused my slumber-producing fantasies toward her. And since I didn't know her, she could be anybody I wanted her to be; for now; in the approach of these visions that were soon to become dreams. I finally closed my eyes.

> Awaiting slumber
> in this refuge called the dark
> Quietly. . .alone. . .

Chapter 11
Intermezzo

Sandy told me about the guys who, he knew for certain, had died. I told Sandy about the guys who, I knew for certain, had died. By the time we finished sharing what we knew, silence prevailed over our realization: he and I were the only ones left alive.

Was this becoming a recurring dream worse than the war itself? I dearly hoped not. Seeing Sandy was supposed to have ended the war—not make it richer in memories and more insistent in making the past become a greater part of my present. My greatest defense against the horror of the war had been my emotional detachment. But this detachment was beginning to dissolve and expose me to the weariness of intense emotion.

Three words had gained a greater and more significant influence on the quality of my existence. The same three words that haunted my presence throughout each day of the war. Three words that now, as a civilian, had a greater meaning for me. Three words: killed in action.

> things don't change
> only one's perspective:
>
> last night's argument
> created grotesque shadows,
> this night's stupor
> leaves all darkness reaching
>
> softer
> always waiting to remember
> the war, you know
> Vietnam can never be

a wonderful place
to take a vacation

*   *   *   *

She had the perfect look, my Catherine—perfectly beautiful. It didn't matter what activity she was engaged in; it didn't matter what she dressed in. It didn't matter because she possessed the most unaffected feminine manner I had ever known in a woman. There was no pretense in her elegant fashion, just a simple economy of movement from point to point. Sexuality was approached in the same manner: delicate but direct, and as passionately as could be imagined.

When it came to cleaning and painting the first home we ever lived in together, it was a joyful expenditure of youthful energy. Ridding our dirty kitchen cabinets of dried insects and pulling off greasy old contact paper from counter tops was an extremely effective method for the quick development of an unpretentious relationship between us. Youth, honesty, naiveté, and our fleeting memories of loneliness were the additional ingredients which strengthened our bond and preserved the veil of romance.

We had no furniture, no heat, and no income; we lacked nothing!

We had a leaky roof, plenty of bad plumbing, and a broken toilet; we lacked everything!

Our golden smiles reflected our riches. And love balanced everything.

So, for three full weeks we played house. That was all the time there was left before Fall Quarter started at Florida State University. Because once school started, we knew that all our time was going to be dedicated to our studies. We were serious students and that was another characteristic that brought us closer together. That and the fact that I laughed at her jokes. It pleased her that I found her amusing. She even admitted that she had a hard time making friends because people always interpreted her behavior as high-strung, difficult, aloof, and humorless.

The purity of her soul made me laugh.

Her inability to tell a lie made me laugh.

The precise method of her rationality made me laugh.

Her generosity made me laugh.

The words she used made me laugh.

Her whole natural being made me laugh so much that I couldn't convince Catherine that I was laughing about her and not at her. I did a lot of laughing in those days. We had nothing. But I felt so wonderfully secure I wanted to shout at the sky.

She never really understood the nature of my laughter. But I couldn't change. The Vietnam War was only a few months behind me and the joy of survival had suddenly become a miracle. All the rest of my life was going to be a gift. . .and I knew it! With this discovery, the measure of my wealth was beyond calculation.

We lived in an old two-bedroom duplex and we spent our first week together cleaning and painting every square foot of the place. On our first day, we worked from morning until night—breaking once for lunch and once for dinner, of Cheese Whiz sandwiches, homemade bread-and-butter pickles, potato chips, and Coca-Cola—because I had a tendency to work without taking a break. Afterward, Catherine insisted on soda breaks and rest periods. She was right, of course. She was right about almost everything concerning our life. And because she loved me so much, I trusted her judgment completely. The war had taken away all my sense of judgment. Up was down and black could be white. Add "I didn't give a damn" to this and you had the formula for a burned-out bush soldier trying to find his way back to the world. Life may have been a gift, yes, but where was the world? I may have been the ship but she was definitely the rudder. And every time my confidence exceeded my ability and I questioned that impeccable judgment of hers, I always fell on my face—each time meeting my ego at that ground level where I would have to pick myself up again and start afresh after an apology she didn't want.

A few days after painting, our no-furniture became a double bed and a dresser in the bedroom, a table and two chairs in the kitchen, and a square overstuffed ottoman with two chairs and a lamp in the living room. All these items had been gathered from our landlord's garage next door. Their condition was worse than second-hand and, in fact, the furniture bordered on junk.

After a few months, no heat meant a fuel oil furnace in the hallway which put out little to no heat. We were cold all winter.

After school started, no money meant one hundred and twenty-five dollars a month from the GI Bill and a thousand dollars worth of school loan money for the Fall Quarter from Catherine's parents, money we later paid back.

By the end of three weeks, the duplex apartment was clean, cozy, and us. Never mind the constant trouble with our plumbing and heating. For me, life had become a paradise of romance amid university surroundings. I was living in the impossible dream. . .because I knew it. Didn't I?

> primordial storm
> accenting the vacant evening
> shadows
>
> standing, swaying,
>
> the surrounding trees
> shivering loudly at making
> wind sounds
>
> standing, swaying,
>
> against the mind and
> not the salient sounds cloaking
> the wind
>
> standing, swaying,
>
> always trembling
> from a consciousness altering
> my thoughts

Chapter 12
"I break easily."

When I awoke, I discovered Frances sitting in the easy chair studying me.

"Did you sleep well?" she asked.

I arose to a sitting position.

"I'm surprised I slept at all," I said. "Where's French?"

"He went grocery shopping."

I shifted my legs off the sofa and planted my feet on the cool terrazzo floor. My eyes were still heavy with sleep.

"Did you make any conclusions?" I asked.

"I don't know enough about you yet."

I smiled.

"You are always direct."

"For a woman with only the shirt on her back, it is either that or sex."

I leaned back on the sofa.

"You learn fast for one night out on the street."

"You forget; there's been a today."

"You don't let anything get by."

It was her turn to smile.

"You're a good sport. You're different," she concluded.

"Why?"

"Most men's egos are fragile."

"I have an ego."

"But you don't wear it on your sleeve like most men."

"I'm trying to get rid of whatever sleeves I've got."

"That's very nice. But you won't succeed."

I presented a quizzical face that expressed an affection for her.

"I like you," I said. "We don't have to have sex."

She got up from her chair.

"We'll see," she said. "I think I'll take a bath."

She unbuckled her belt as she started to leave.

"Fran."

"Llew?"

"I'll get your clothes from him," I said.

"I won't put your life in danger."

"You already have."

She hesitated. Her eyes fluttered introspectively as she bit her lower lip.

"Please. Don't pull on me too hard. Not yet. I break. I break easily."

Our eyes connected in a moment of intensity: her eyes registering vulnerability and my eyes registering compassion. She limped out of the living room cradling her injured left arm in her right and disappeared down the hallway toward the bathroom. I retained her image by closing my eyes:

> our touching
> ever so gently
> with leftover pain

Chapter 13
"Long story."

They blew into the living room like a whirlwind: Willie, Janet and Tommie. They blew in through the front door without a key, since French usually left the door unlocked, and they blew in as if this was a regular and natural occurrence. Their faces brightened with their discovery of me.

"It's true!" Willie exclaimed.

Janet skirted around Willie and Tommie and gave me a hug just as I got up from the sofa.

"Where the hell have you been?" she asked.

"Where Llew has never been before," I answered.

She kissed me on the cheek.

"It's good to see you," Tommie finally said in his usual quiet manner. He took another step in my direction while I stepped around Janet to meet him halfway. We stopped further progress toward each other with a handshake and a gentle focus, eye to eye.

Tommie, the quiet one. Tommie, the blond-headed, blue-eyed, pretty boy with an uncertain future because he was unable to shake off his uncertain past; a past marked with poverty, ignorance, and white-trash squalor; a past he had managed to rise above but one that haunted and even crippled his judgment.

Willie severed our handshake with his usual stampede of gregariousness which always placed him at the center of attention. This was accomplished by a boisterous hug which encouraged Tommie to move aside. A pat on my back followed his hug along with a barrage of euphemisms that, when distilled, meant he was glad to see me.

Willie had gained weight. In fact, he was outright chubby. A flabby tire of excess flesh traveled the complete circumference of his waist, drooping over the upper rim of his belt. He was out of shape, but he still carried himself in the manner of a young man posing like a peacock for women: stomach in, chest out, and biceps slightly flexed. He walked with an embarrassing swagger which accentuated the present condition of his five-foot, ten-inch frame. But through it all, Willie had an appealing smile which no one could resist. His smile was further enhanced by a pair of equally appealing eyes that were enclosed by a set of pinched eyelids. The darkness of his eyes and the ruddiness of his complexion produced an exotic appearance. His greatest attribute, however, was his dazzling gift for gab. And if that wasn't enough to fool you into thinking you were in the company of a man of substance, there was that secret glint he always wore which made you feel you were sharing a secret with him. Even though nobody knew or ever challenged him on what that secret was.

But in the final analysis, Willie was a fake. He was a liar and a cheat if he knew he could get away with it. And one could faithfully count upon his untrustworthiness. In spite of all this, people loved Willie, although they never liked him in their day-to-day dealings with him.

I had to like him, hug him, and even share his non-secret with him. I always did. I was doing those things with him now.

"What's your no good?" Willie asked as we kept a firm hand-shake between us. That's all he said. I was surprised. Expectant. By now he should have been well into a discourse on his latest scheme. At least throwing a line of bullshit my way. The gleam in his eyes turned into gold, then into amber, then into the dark brown that were his eyes. Tired eyes. Willie had changed. He looked older than his age.

"Speak English, Will."

"Okay. You look like shit. How come?"

I didn't answer his question. And I was just as cruel.

"You've put on weight."

Willie finally released his grip and pulled his hand out of our handshake as he stepped back. He raised both hands up to his midriff and pinched the bulge on either side of himself.

"Love handles, baby. These are love handles."

"French told me you joined the Marine Corps," I said.

"I did," Willie said.

"Willie's AWOL."

"Shut up, Janet." Willie caught himself. "I'm sorry, honey."

Janet seemed to be unaffected. But now I noticed that she, too, looked tired. As tired as Willie looked; as Tommie looked; as I must have looked.

"What's happened to us?" I finally said.

"What do you mean?" Tommie asked.

"Nothing." I couldn't explain.

"No, we're not kids anymore, big boy," Willie said, completing the circuit of my thoughts. "None of us are rocket scientists." He smiled. "Let's face it. All of us, put together, will never split an atom."

"But one of us can fix a drink," Janet chided, already bored with the metaphysical direction our conversation was leading. She appeared to be annoyed with Willie. Tired of the thoughts that had apparently brought his life to a standstill. It was written in her slump-shouldered manner, her indifference toward the development of this conversation. She had changed, too.

"Tom, would you get that bottle of bourbon out of the car for me, please?" she asked.

"Sure thing," he answered as he turned himself toward the front door and carried out her request.

I had this sense that she had accepted life as it was, as it is. . .nothing more, nothing less.

Had she discovered something? I wondered. It wasn't love. Not from or for Willie. How did I know that?

I watched her disappear into the kitchen to set up the glasses with ice for a round of drinks. There was nothing between Willie and me now. Our facades crumbled.

"I've thought about you a lot," Willie said.

"I wish I could say the same." I was being honest. "But I am glad to see you."

"Changed. It's all changed."

"What? Miami?"

Willie sneered cynically.

"Yeah. Miami." His eyes shifted away momentarily. When they refocused in my direction, they had no luster and no humor within them. "Can I trust you?" I nodded. He stepped toward me. Intimately. Desperately. "I think I want to kill myself." I remained quiet. "I don't know why. I'm empty, Llew. What does that mean?"

"What do you want?"

"Hell, I don't know." He stepped away in agitation breaking the bond of our intimacy. "I've thought myself into a corner. I'm trapped, man. I'm suffocating. I can't stand the pain anymore."

I wished I could have told him that emptiness was all there was. That all he had to do was look into that emptiness, that self, for his happiness. I'd only caught a glimpse of it. But I'd actually seen it in Jansen. I knew it existed; happiness was as good a word for it as any. A word, I know, but a good one. Willie had been watching me think.

"Are you happy, Llew?"

I waved my hand at him in a declaration of uncertainty.

"Long story, Will. Long story."

"I haven't got much time," he said.

I noticed Tommie standing to one side, cradling a narrow brown paper bag in his right arm. There was no telling how long he'd been standing there.

"I'm back," Tommie said quietly. The tone of his voice was apologetic. His intrusion had been noted.

Willie's face became animated once again. His untruthful smile had returned.

"And glad to have you back, my boy."

Tommie knew he was lying. But he didn't care. What concerned Tommie was his intrusion. That's because Tommie never felt comfortable around people. Even with people he knew, he had to be primed like a hand pump. And like water having to be used each time to draw water up from the well of an old hand pump, so was Tommie's inclination toward withdrawal from human interaction. The air of human behavior always stirred uneasily around Tommie. And it always radiated an uneasy feeling which contaminated the senses of those meeting him for the first time and every time thereafter. Nobody was immune to this odd aura of his. People shied away from him because of it and friends consciously tolerated it. As a consequence, he was a loner in the extreme sense of the word, to the degree that he was lonely. This condition of self was not of his choosing. He'd been born that way: a good looking man trapped within a eerie persona. There was nothing Tommie could do about this. He knew that. And he knew he had to keep what friends he had or withdraw into oblivion.

"For Christ sake, Tom," Willie said somewhat irritably. "Loosen up."

Tommie raised the package he was carrying in an effort to

appear casual.

"I am loose, see?"

Tommie didn't wait for Willie to amplify his attack and scooted into the kitchen to help Janet. Willie turned to me and noted my perplexity.

"Long story," he said to me. "Long story."

Chapter 14
"One of us."

The bathroom door was unlocked. Not by design, but because the lock was broken. And since French usually lived alone, he never felt compelled to fix it. This is why Janet accidently intruded upon Frances's privacy in the bathroom.

"Go away!" Frances shouted.

I could hear her shrill voice. Its intensity had traveled down the hallway. Janet shrieked in response.

"Llew! Come here! Quickly!"

I needed no explanation from Janet when I reached the open bathroom door. Frances had been caught in the act of attempting suicide. Her left wrist had been slit open. Her right hand still held the double-edged razor blade. The truth of her intent was magnified by the blood spattered on the white porcelain sink.

I resisted my first impulse to cry out with indignation.

This woman was not kidding around, I thought. She needed the tone of rationality.

"Frances, this is Janet. Janet. . .Frances."

Frances looked at me dumbfoundedly in response to my casual introduction. She made every attempt to digest my words. And when it became apparent to me that she was unable to decipher what I had said, she looked at her wrist and began to laugh. The razor blade tumbled out of her right hand and clinked into the bloody sink. In a domino effect, she bent forward into the sink as her laughter turned into a hysteria of tears. Her legs buckled and she crumbled to her knees.

Janet had been very still. She had been astute enough to remain quiet, to disappear from the moment and not encourage Fran's potential for violence against herself.

I grabbed a towel from a rack as I brushed past Janet and approached Frances.

"Jesus Christ," Janet finally said to me in a whisper. "Who is she?"

"One of us," I said. "Give me a hand."

By this time, Willie and Tommie were in the hallway peering into the bathroom. Neither one of them said anything. They knew their words would only crowd this impossible situation.

In direct contrast to Fran's limp arm, her emotional tension increased when she felt the contact of my hands. She did not resist me, nor did she resist Janet's support from behind. I began to wrap her left wrist with the towel.

"He hurt your right arm and now you've hurt your left."

"Leave me alone," she lamented.

"Come on, honey," Janet whispered to Frances in her most compassionate tone. "Let me help you up."

"I don't want any help!" she screamed. Then Frances slumped onto her rear end, making it more impossible in that confined bathroom. Her action pushed Janet backward a little, forcing her to sit on the edge of the bathtub. The three of us were hopelessly congested in the middle of a triad of bathroom fixtures: the sink, the toilet, and that bathtub. Frances finally noticed Willie and Tommie peering through the doorway.

"What are they doing here!" she spat with anger, resentful of her forced publicity.

I waved at them vehemently to get away from the door. But like most innocent bystanders, they hesitated until I had to say the words.

"Will you two get the hell out of here?"

The irritation in my voice was the only thing that wasn't ignored. They looked at each other as if I were crazy; even mimicked my displeasure. I was still applying direct pressure around her wrist when I felt a slight downward pull. Her sobbing had become deeply spasmodic and she gulped for air in between each word she spoke.

"I want to die."

"What the hell has she been smoking?" Willie commented insensitively.

"Willie, shut up," Janet countered. "Himself. That's all he thinks about. Men. Egos as fragile as glass. And so big, they can't consider anyone else's feelings."

Willie feigned innocence. "What did I do?" He looked at Tommie for support. He got silence and neutrality.

"That's right, stick together," Janet persisted.

The situation was becoming hopeless. I looked at Tommie for help. He understood my non-verbal plea and stepped inside to assist me. I shifted behind Frances, forcing Janet to step completely into the bathtub, while Tommie took my place in front of Frances. Tommie gathered her legs, one in each of his hands, as I hooked my arms up under her armpits. Together we lifted her off the floor. Janet and Willie continued their low-grade argument as we shuffled out of the bathroom.

"Be careful, Tom. There's a lot of blood on this tile," I said as I slipped but managed to recover before I fell.

"You okay?" Tommie asked.

"Yeah, I've got her. Go ahead. Keep going."

Tommie backed out into the hallway and allowed me to pivot in the direction of my choosing as soon as I cleared the bathroom door. I would have liked to have backed my way into our bedroom, laid her down on the bed, and closed the door on the whole matter. But I knew that was not possible. The towel around Fran's wrist was soaked with blood. This had been no dramatic display for attention. Frances had had every intention of killing herself.

"This way, Tom. Let's put her on the living room sofa." Willie and Janet's domestic squabbling was beginning to get on my nerves. "Will you two shut up!" Their silence was abrupt. "Willie, call for an ambulance. Janet, go to the kitchen and bring me the sharpest knife you can find."

Guilt prevailed and they proceeded to follow my instructions with haste. Tommie and I placed Frances on the couch.

"Okay, Tom. Thanks. Now would you mind very much cleaning up the bathroom while I watch over her?"

"Sure thing."

I was about to explain the reason for my request when he verbally stopped me.

"I understand. What else can I do?"

"Get me another towel."

"Right."

"And do a good job in there, man," I said to him as he directed himself back to the bathroom.

"Don't worry," he said.

Willie bounced back into the living room with Janet trailing after him.

"The ambulance is on its way," Willie announced after having dialed 911 on the kitchen wallphone.

"This is the best I can do," Janet said while offering me a long, stainless steel, serrated knife.

"That will do," I said as I took it from her. "Tom, where's that towel?"

He appeared, like magic, and tossed a white towel at me.

"Here you go."

Willie caught it and handed the towel to me.

"Thanks," I said to both of them.

Tommie disappeared down the hallway to finish cleaning the bathroom as I began to unwrap the blood-soaked towel around Fran's wrist.

"Willie, I want you to take this towel into the kitchen and I want you to smear her blood on the counter and in the sink. Find a cutting board and get something out of the refrigerator. Anything. Make it look like an accident." I handed him the bloody towel. "Go on." I then cradled Fran's wrist in the clean white towel I had and smeared the serrated knife with her blood. I ran the flat of the knife, on both sides, across her cut and I presented the knife to Janet. "Here. Take this back into the kitchen. Set the whole thing up. You know what to do."

"Okay," she said.

She went into the kitchen.

"Why are you doing this?" Frances finally asked as I wrapped the clean towel tightly around her wrist.

"Breakfast would be no fun without you anymore."

She almost smiled. It was the first break in her tragic composure. Her head fell back against the sofa's backrest in a resigned attitude.

"What did I do to deserve you?" she mumbled irritably.

"You ran out of cigarettes, remember?"

Chapter 15
Everything In Common

By the time we returned from the hospital, the evening's darkness had descended upon us. The staff had been suspicious about the cause of the injury but they did not press the issue. Frances had performed surprisingly well and eventually convinced them that it had been a perfectly normal accident. With Frances in bed asleep, the five of us, Willie, Janet, Tommie, French and I, sat at the kitchen table nursing our well-deserved beers.

"I couldn't believe it when Willie told me what Frances did to herself," French finally declared.

"Thanks for picking us up at the hospital, Will," I interjected.

Janet and I had accompanied Frances to the hospital in the ambulance. We had left Willie and Tommie behind to inform French of what had happened. Then they drove to Baptist Hospital's emergency room and picked us up in Willie's Mustang.

"Is she crazy?" French asked with genuine concern.

"Of course not," I said in her defense.

"She only tried to commit suicide," Willie said. "I like her."

"And I suppose I could say the same thing about you," Janet said to Willie, in her first attempt to warm up to him since their argument earlier that day.

"Oh, but you love me. That means I'm going to succeed when I decide to do it," Willie said.

French was utterly bewildered.

"All I did was go out for groceries," French innocently announced. The four of us laughed.

"Where did you pick her up, Llew?" Janet asked.

"She picked me up. No. Actually, we picked each other up."

"Does that mean you two have a lot in common?" Janet teased.

"She tried to kill herself," Willie said. "We have everything in common."

"You're awfully quiet, Tom," I said.

"Just thinking," he said. We all waited for him to complete his thought. One always had to wait for Tommie to complete a thought. "I don't know if I should be sorry. . .over how much we've changed."

"She's not one of us," French interjected.

"She is now," I said. I got up from my chair. "Hey, guys, I'm tired. It's been a very long day for me."

Then it occurred to me that Tommie was supposed to be moving in with French. "Frances and I will be out of here tomorrow morning. Okay Tom? French?"

"Like hell," Tommie said. "Where are you going? I can make myself comfortable in the living room for as long as it takes. Right, French?"

"I don't mind if you don't mind," French shrugged without concern.

"Sure. It'll be like one big happy family."

"Thanks, Tom. I owe you one," I said.

"And don't forget us, partner," Willie added. "Janet and I are renting a duplex just off of Lejune Road near Miracle Mile. Any of you are always welcome to spend the night if you get sick of each other here."

"Although I don't know how long we can extend that welcome since we're three months behind in our rent," Janet caustically added.

Willie's eyes focused sharply upon her with anger but he remained silent.

"So. . .does this mean that we're trying to become one big happy family?" I asked to dissipate some of the tension.

"I guess," French agreed.

"Now all we have to do is find out which one of us is the happy one," Willie added with his usual sense of conspiracy reflected in his eyes, ". . .and kill him."

Chapter 16
The Moon

I couldn't sleep that night. I tried. But I tossed and turned until my restlessness finally succeeded in waking Frances up.

"I'm sorry."

"Don't be."

She sat up and lit a cigarette. We remained quiet for a long time. Long enough for Frances to light another cigarette.

"What do you believe in, Llew?"

I got off the bed and walked over to the window to look outside. The moon greeted me. It made me happy. And for a brief moment, I forgot myself. I looked at the moon until I had an answer for her. The moon:

> Halting. Perceiving
> once again, I must ask:
> Have you always been there
> every time I've raised my head toward
>   your brilliant face?
> every time the sky has become
>   less dark with your presence?
> every time you appear, when I'm suddenly
>   ready to see you? I look up
> and wonder:
> Where did you suddenly come from?
> You're so pure and beautiful.
> Why hadn't I noticed you?
> again
> Why must I call you?
> The moon
> Why must I be I, every time
>   I don't see your face?
> And what are you when you're suddenly seen

> and I'm not suddenly I?
> Are you really the moon? Or is it I?
> suddenly
> again
> looking at the sky. . .

She crushed out her cigarette and rolled over onto her side facing away from me. I listened to the silence between us. After a while, I heard the sound of crying accent the darkness.

"Are you going to be alright?"

"I don't know. Yes," she said irritably.

"Tomorrow. . .I think I'm going to look for a job."

"So, what am I supposed to do about that?" she answered curtly.

"Nothing. Can I trust you?"

"To do what?"

"Not to hurt yourself."

"No. But I do want to be alone." She turned back around to me after she wiped away her tears. "And I won't kill myself while you're gone tomorrow, I promise," she said. Then she turned away from me again and threw herself against her pillow. This time there were no tears, just a dark silence.

Chapter 17
Half of a Half Lotus

Fran's breathing had become shallow and regular. I had remained by the window peering through the darkness that was surrounding me. I couldn't sleep. I looked at the moon and asked myself, "But where is my Zen? My Zen?"

I knew it was here, with me. But where? It was easy to use words to try to comfort Frances. And why weren't these same words comforting me? Why couldn't I listen to my own advice? Was I lying to her? And myself? These questions disturbed me. The I that was myself felt intangible. Suddenly, I shuddered without joy or sadness. It was simply a physical reaction to my next thought: perhaps that "I" was not myself. The abruptness of this realization did not startle me. I felt different. I was not afraid of this thought.

I ran my fingers through my wet hair. I was sweating profusely in spite of the central air conditioning. I felt out of sync and yet. . .

I quietly approached the bed and plucked my pillow from it without disturbing Frances. Then I folded the pillow in half, placed it on the floor, and sat down on it to do zazen. It was the only solution to my predicament; the only answer to my questions; the only correct response to what I was presently experiencing.

I managed to cross my legs into a modified half lotus position: my left ankle was under my right thigh and my right ankle crossed over the top of my left calf instead of my left thigh. I had improved my posture tremendously since the first time I started doing zazen. Half of a half lotus: this was the best that I could do and, therefore, this was perfect.

I smiled at myself. This was something I had not done since my companionship with Jansen. He had shown me this perfection time and time again; even in his death.

I placed my hands in the mudra position, straightened my back, lifted the top of my head toward the sky, tucked in my chin and began to concentrate on my breathing.

"Watch your tanden. It lies just below your naval. Your breath originates there. You originate there. Good." Jansen laughed. Jansen had never left me.

the aloneness. . .
in discovering
the universe

Chapter 18
Intermezzo

I had no guilt. Sandy had no innocence. I had nothing to forget. Sandy had everything to remember: just one small, minor, atrocity; a harmless mutilation, really—"the man was already dead!" he said. And mutilation was the most definite way to confirm an enemy kill. So, he cut off one of the dead man's fingers. A minor sin. A venial sin amid one that had been a mortal. Nobody had been there to judge him. Nobody but Sandy and—if he believed in a supreme being—God.

Had he been able to live with his guilt? No. Have others been able to? No.

Statistics addressing this problem have been illuminating; our losses through suicide have said it all. To date, 60,000 Vietnam Veterans have put a gun to their own head to escape some form of guilt.

Did these suicides occur after the war? Or were these deaths a continuation of the war? Thinking and thoughts, over and over, "Is it over?"

Will the war ever end?

vacant shadows attending
reoccurring dreams about the war

first thought in the morning
last thought in the evening (muted sounds;
rapid small arms fire
all day long)

frozen photographs about childish laughter;
about boys becoming men

frozen memories all day long
all day long

vacant shadows, reoccurring dreams,
year after year after year

*   *   *   *

Our dining room was small and sparse and managed to be the most important room in our home. The dining room was centrally located and had doorways leading out into a living room, a kitchen, a bathroom, a bedroom, and a hallway which led to the master bedroom—five doorways in all. It was the one room that had to be entered to get anywhere else in our home, except for the main entrance into the duplex which led directly into the living room.

In the winter, this room was the warmest place to be and in the summer it was the most comfortable. There were only two straight-backed chairs and a scarred wooden table that had been brush-coated with white enamel paint sometime during the early part of the twentieth century. To cover the discolored and chipped paint and to lessen the effects of the gouged table top, a vinyl table cloth with a heavy cotton backing was required to make it presentable for eating and serviceable for studying. Which is also why this room became the heart of our home.

We did everything but sleep in this room. And although making love, in the physical sense, was the only other important activity reserved for the bedroom, we made love in every other way in the dining room: kissing, touching, dreaming, studying, eating, laughing, talking, hugging.

The dining room was also the place where Catherine learned how not to cook; where she learned that it wasn't required of her just because she was a woman; where she realized I truly considered her an equal and not a maid or a cook or a laundress. She was my colleague, my lover, my beautiful woman, my friend. But it takes two people to comprehend equality before equality can be understood between two people. It became understood even though we had become husband and wife because, luckily, the two of us required the expression of individuality. And this manifested itself through the destruction of any male/female role playing and through the deep respect we had for one another. The initial foundation for this destruction came about quite innocently and undramatically.

The incident occurred soon after we had established our home and were enrolled in the Fall Quarter at Florida State University. And it was during our initial school week together, when our first sense of a routine was being organized, when I noticed that Catherine was involving herself entirely too much in the kitchen. She was cooking extravagant meals that were wonderful but, frankly, too much. I had long been used to a simpler fare: a sandwich or a little soup or something out of a can or a simple bowl of rice with a few beans—just something to eat. Catherine was presenting me with meat and potatoes and stewed tomatoes and corn and broccoli and salad and even rolls! Leftovers was a concept I attributed to my parents. Anyway, it was a small thing but small things often become big things. And the big thing was our future, our careers, our lives as students in an academic world. It had to be made clear that we had a responsibility to ourselves not to sacrifice what we were before we became we. I wanted Catherine to remain the Catherine I fell in love with and Catherine felt the same way about me. Together, we wanted to evolve as individuals rather than dissolve ourselves into one another. This was an intellectual perspective.

I looked up at her from the dining room table, with a lavish meal spread before me, and said, "This is not required. This is unnecessary. We are not our parents."

She immediately understood. In fact, I detected a sigh of relief, a realization. She sat down; something within her had momentarily stopped. From that point on, the equality between us became a concrete part of our behavior and not merely a concept.

> the silence within, stirring
> with circular thoughts
> spinning. spinning
> into a standstill—
> is this thinking?
> (no, it is midnight)
> and this is another dissection, "into

the subconscious"
is in a stalemate:

thinking. thinking
why shouldn't it be?
a silent rhapsody
why shouldn't there be?
two dogs barking

Chapter 19
Cash

The light of daybreak had awakened me. And even though I had only slept a few short hours, I felt refreshed.

I took a cool shower, got dressed, and then ambled over to the kitchen, where I hovered over a cup of coffee for a long time. Within the next hour, Tommie and French performed the same morning ritual. We eventually had a breakfast of toast and jelly together. Frances slept through it all.

French stood up from his chair after he finished the last of his coffee. "Well, gotta go."

Tommie got up as abruptly as French.

"Yeah, me too. I'm working a double shift at the station today."

"I'm going with you, French."

"What for?"

"To get a job."

"What do you know about drafting?"

"Not with you, silly."

"Then with who?"

"I'm not sure."

"We have a high turnover at the Robo Gas Station where I work." Tommie interjected. "I can let you know when there's an opening."

"Thanks, Tom. But in the meantime, it won't hurt for me to look around this morning."

"Suit yourself," French said. "You don't have to worry."

"I know, French."

"Well then, come on. I don't want to be late for work."

I sat quietly with French looking out the car window. French and Tommie had driven away in opposite directions.

"Tom doesn't know what he's doing with his life," French confided as he made a right turn at the corner.

"Neither do I," I confessed.

"Somehow I don't believe that."

"Why?"

"You're not helpless. Because no matter what, you know how to survive. You have the will to live. At the very least, you're searching for something important."

"And that's how I appear to you?"

"I meant all that as a compliment."

"And so it was taken. But you give me more credit than I deserve."

"I knew you were going to say something like that. See what I mean? I expect things like that from you." A short silence separated us before French continued. "Tommie is a good guy."

"I know."

"Then you'll help me straighten him out? He needs someone to push him in the right direction."

"I won't stop you."

French smiled.

"You're a character, Llewellen."

My smile reflected his; I kept my silence.

I looked out the car window again and noticed someone on a riding lawn mower cutting the grass of a very large lawn in front of an office complex.

"French, pull over."

"What?"

"Pull over."

I got out of the car as soon as it came to a stop.

"I've got an idea for a job. I'll see you tonight."

"What are you doing? Are you sure?"

"Don't worry about me."

"Okay," he said a little skeptically. But he was amused and waved a hand good naturedly at me, as he always did. "Take care of yourself. See you tonight."

I waited for French to disappear before making a careful approach toward the lawn man on the riding mower. I kept a respectable distance from him but remained close enough to indicate that I was interested in something. He openly glared at me a number of times. And after several passes on his lawn mower, he stopped the mower in front me.

"What are you looking for?" he croaked with a frog-like voice.

"A job," I answered.

"Is that so?"The man leaned over the other side of the mower and discharged a wad of brown spittle. It shot out of his mouth like a projectile and landed on the ground several feet away from us. I could tell I had his undivided attention. He took another moment to size me up before he spoke. "I'll pay you three dollars an hour."

He stepped down off his riding lawn mower like you would a horse.

"Now?" I said.

"I can play, too," he said.

"I'm not playing."

"Then this will give me a chance to see you work a few hours. I'll do the trimming while you ride. Know how to drive one of these things?" I nodded. "Good. I pay at the end of a job each day. Cash. No names. No questions asked."

"But my name is Llew," I said in the manner that told him I had nothing to hide.

"So your name is Llew. Let's see what you can do."

We worked all morning without a break. As soon as we had finished the first job, we moved on to other jobs, residential as well as commercial. We stayed in the southwest section of Miami.

The man had a riding mower, a push mower, an edger, and a Weed-Whacker. He transported this entire ensemble in the back of an open trailer he towed with a pickup truck. The trailer was made of wood and the gate in the rear folded down to provide a ramp for the on- and off-loading of the equipment. The entire rig, truck and trailer, was clean and well organized. And it was a positive reflection of the owner, who was also clean and well organized. He was short, stocky, and powerfully built. His neck was as big as one of my thighs. The features of his almost malformed face were pinched close together and painted a leathery brown like the rest of the exposed skin on his body, especially on the back of his neck. He spoke little. But when he did, his voice was deep and throaty-sounding like a croaking bullfrog. He chewed lots of tobacco and his left cheek bulged as if it had a tumor.

It was hot as hell and I was glad to be inside the cab of the pickup truck going to the next job. I swore I wouldn't be caught out there tomorrow without my bamboo hat. That is, if there was going to be a tomorrow. The lawn mower man drove into the parking lot of a donut shop on Bird Road. He reached into his pocket, pulled out some money, and counted out nineteen dollars and fifty cents. It was one-thirty in the afternoon and we had worked steadily since seven that morning. He handed me the money.

"Can you be here at ten tomorrow morning?"

"Sure," I said. It was within walking distance of French's house, I happily thought.

"I've got a couple of small jobs to do in the northwest section before I pick you up. I won't be here if you're late."

"I'll be here."

"Good."

I got out of the truck and said thanks. He nodded as he let off on the brake and started inching away from me. Then he reapplied the brakes and came to a complete stop again. He hesitated before he looked at me and said, "You can call me Ted."

"Thanks for the job, Ted."

He drove away responding to my gratitude with a grunt and headed down Bird Road toward Coral Gables. I put the money I had earned into my pocket. I was tired. I was hot. But I was happy.

I started for home by crossing Bird Road. The heat of the pavement and the black tar rose vertically in visible waves. It was only the end of April and already the Miami heat was stifling. To think, it wasn't long ago that I was complaining about the cold in Baltimore. Now it was the heat. I checked myself. No. I was not going to complain. I was happy, remember? I had cash in my pocket.

    visible
    through squinting eyes. . .
    highway fumes

Chapter 20
"We're all idiots."

The Red Diamond Inn was a hole-in-the-wall establishment located at the center of a strip mall of worn-out shops. There was nothing exceptionally inviting about its exterior and if I had been driving by it, I would not have noticed it at all. But one's perspective changes dramatically when one walks in a world almost exclusively built for driving; a world with no sidewalks, no shade, no crosswalks, no human consideration at all. It is a world where main streets have too many lanes, and the ones that don't are either under construction or scheduled for widening in the near future.

The highway is a dusty, compassionless world where the pedestrian is at a decided disadvantage. Automobiles viciously speed along without any thought of the consequences of their actions. I say automobiles because the people who drive them are no longer people. They are entities so busy rushing around to save five minutes that they have lost all perspective, all value for life treading along the side of the road. People on foot are considered no better than dogs or cats or unsuspecting wildlife. By their definition, a lesser animal is any animal not behind the wheel of a car.

"I will not swerve my car away from you," they'll think. "I'm in a hurry. You're a nuisance on this side of the road."

I feel sorry for dogs and cats and wildlife. I feel sorry for those entities who are the lost parts of ourselves. We have not risen to meet the advance of this technology. Instead, we have pulled that technology down to match our baser instincts.

Okay. Alright. I confess. I did not discover the Red Diamond Inn through any great powers of observation. It was my stepping away from the perilous approach of several vehicles which had a lot to do with this. I wanted to be mad. I wanted to shake my fist at them. But the drivers of those vehicles didn't even bother to look into their rearview mirrors. It was my job to get out of their way.

"Idiots," I said to myself. "We're all idiots."

> open highway. . .
> the primitiveness in people
> as they drive

I needed to get away from the heat and the traffic's exhaust fumes. I decided I wanted a beer and this was as good a place as any to get one. I opened the front door and entered.

I hesitated in the relative darkness before taking a seat at the bar. The only three things the place had to offer, I wanted. It was quiet, it was cool, and the draft beer was cold. This was good. And this was enough. . .to get me home.

Chapter 21
"Oo, nasty."

I got back home around three o'clock in the afternoon. French and Tommie were still at work. Frances was in the living room watching a soap opera on television.

She was huddled at one end of the sofa with both her knees bent upward toward her chest. She glanced at me and quickly repositioned herself to hide her bandaged wrist. She stared at the television.

"Do you feel up to buying a change of clothes?" I asked. She didn't answer me. "We'll have to buy them at a thrift shop. It's what I can afford right now," I said, ignoring her silence.

"Sure. If you want to," she finally said. She didn't seem to mind the idea of thrift shop clothes.

"Good," I said. And by the time I took a shower, changed clothes, and located a thrift shop in the phone book that was within walking distance, she was ready.

The interlude between the air conditioning of the house and the air conditioning of the thrift shop was hot, humid, and sweaty. The traffic was as threatening as ever.

Once inside the thrift shop, we managed to find her two pairs of blue jeans and three tee shirts.

There was a glint of happiness in her eyes when she walked out of the shop with her new clothes neatly folded into a white plastic bag. But that glint was suddenly erased and replaced by a set of fearful eyes which focused upon a passing vehicle with two guys glaring at her. One of them took note of me while the other honked the horn at her. But they didn't stop. I was unable to get a good look at them.

"Is that him?" I asked.

"Yes. Let's hurry."

"No. We're not running."

"Please. You don't know him."

"He won't be back. He's a coward."

I knew that for sure, now: the adolescent honk; the quality of the glare; the revving of the engine.

I held her steady by the arm. I was determined not to move, determined to prove to her that I was right. A few minutes went by without any results.

"How about a beer," I said.

She was completely occupied with her thoughts.

"I'm buying," I added.

"You must really want to get into my pants," she finally conceded in an attempt at humor.

"Oo, nasty. Talk like that doesn't count unless it's over a beer," I said with a friendly smirk. "Come on. There's this place down the street. The Red Diamond Inn. It's dark and it's quiet. We don't even have to talk."

Chapter 22
No Closer to Enlightenment

Sunset greeted Frances and me when we stepped out of the Red Diamond Inn. The effect of too many beers had us glowing with happiness. We glided back to French's house unaware of the dangers surrounding us except for one incident. And that was when I had to snatch Frances off the street by one of her arms because she almost stepped in front of a car.

Everybody was at French's house by the time we got there.

"Where have you two been?" Willie demanded.

"Shopping!" Frances answered brightly, as she limped over to Janet to show her the new clothes. I'd forgotten about her slight limp until now. Funny. Their presence changed everything.

"I got a job," I said.

"He got a job," Willie mimicked to Janet.

"This calls for a celebration," French declared as he pitched two beers at me, one at a time. I gave one to Frances.

Laughter among friends was the next sound I recognized. The pure, simple, half-in-the-bag laughter of an ordinary party. But the sounds were a lie. Nobody was really here. Everyone's thoughts were elsewhere. Each of them was looking in one direction yet thinking in another. The eyes reflecting their inner voice betrayed them all: the deep melancholy of Willie, the childlike confusion of Tommie, the growing hardness in Janet, and the low self-esteem in Frances. I wasn't sure about French. I couldn't understand what he was getting out of all this. And as for myself, where was I? These very thoughts were the reflection of my own lack of presence. I was no better off than any of them. No closer to enlightenment. I sought some comfort in the thought that perhaps I was also no further away. Still, where was I?

"It's boys' night out," Willie declared emphatically. "We'll go in my car."

"Not on your life," Janet pounced. "There's no way Frances and I are staying home while you guys play."

"French, get her off my ass and lend her your car," Willie pleaded.

French tossed Janet his keys without a drop of protest.

"Free at last," Willie dramatically proclaimed. "Let's go."

After I caught Janet's attention, I glanced over to Frances to communicate my concern for her. Frances observed this silent interchange. She slunk back a few steps and circled around to my left until she disappeared from my peripheral vision. She pressed herself against me from behind to manifest her presence once again. She whispered into my ear. But Willie could also hear her words.

"Stop treating me like a kid. I'll be fine," she said, then facetiously, "I promise I won't try to kill myself tonight."

Chapter 23
Control

Chrome Avenue was dark. The road was still under construction and it came to a dead end at one edge of the Everglades; what was left of the Glades.

"But I won't promise," Willie flatly stated as he drove. Tommie and French were sitting in the back and I was sitting in the front with Willie. I assumed he was addressing me. But I did not ask him to amplify his statement. I turned to him and waited. He spoke.

"I won't promise not to try and kill myself tonight."

I wasn't sure if he was mimicking Frances or not. I reserved my judgment—and my anger. He continued.

"I'm not kidding, Llew."

He stepped on the gas, forcing the car to accelerate dangerously. And before any of us had the chance to become alarmed, Willie hit the brakes and pulled the wheel hard to the left. His red two-door Mustang spun one hundred and eighty degrees and stalled out when it came to a stop.

"Jesus!" French shouted. "You could have gotten us all killed!"

"Are you alright, Willie?" I asked.

"No," he answered with both hands on the wheel.

"I'm going to stay with you all the way," I said, firmly resolved to see whatever was going to happen through to the end.

Willie reached for the keys and started the car again.

"Not me," French said as he indicated for me to open the door on my side to let him out. "I'll wait for you right here until you're all finished doing whatever it is you're doing."

"I'm coming with you," Tommie said as he slid across the back seat to get out.

"Bring a six-pack with you, Tom," French said as he turned away. "Glad somebody around here has some sense," he mumbled to himself.

Willie wasn't listening. He was waiting. As soon as Tommie slammed the door shut, Willie pressed down on the accelerator with his foot and skidded the car away, leaving a small trail of burned rubber on the pavement and black smoke in the air. Then the rear of the car fishtailed in a zigzag motion until the tires gripped the road. The noise which accompanied all this momentarily frightened me; I was concerned about Tommie and French. I turned to Willie as soon as I was sure they were safely clear from us.

"Do anything you want. Kill yourself. But not at someone else's expense."

"What difference does it make?" he said.

Willie had reached a desired speed. And without hesitation, he cut the wheel hard again, sending the Mustang into a spin. The engine stalled as the car rocked to a standstill. A moment of silence passed between us before Willie spoke.

"This car should have rolled over that time."

I took a deep breath and noted our position. We were facing in the same direction of travel but were no longer parallel to the road. The Mustang's engine had stalled out again. He started to reach for the keys but I quickly placed my hand over them to buy a few moments of his attention. He looked at me. I continued to speak calmly.

"Anything. You can do anything as long as you don't harm someone else. That's your moral obligation. That's. . ." I almost said "enlightenment" when I suddenly remembered an expression I once heard. It was a working definition for individuality embodied in three clear words. "That's. . .enlightened self-interest." He slid his hand under mine and started the car again. "You're not listening to me, Will."

"Are you in for the ride or not?" he stated flatly.

I quietly leaned back into my seat and waited. He pushed the gas pedal all the way to the floor. The cosmos of the night surrounding me became almost tangible, almost like dust. I knew I was near death. The wheel went down. We swerved to the left. Spun. Stopped. Stalled into silence.

Willie began to cry.

"I'm so unhappy, Llew."

I was hesitant.

"What do you want, Will?"

He looked at me. Tears were streaming from his eyes.

"I don't know," he said. "How can I know if I don't know who I am?"

"Then look within yourself," I said.

"That's not important."

"It's everything."

"But there's nothing there."

"That's right."

Willie blew his nose into a handkerchief.

"You don't make any sense," he said.

"Death is also an attachment."

I reached into the back seat and pulled two cans of beer out of a bag. I opened them and handed him one. We both drank deeply.

"You want me to drive?" I asked.

"No. It's okay." He started the car again and made a U-turn. "You were right about French and Tommie."

"That's a start," I said politely.

"No. It just changes the end."

By this time we were almost alongside French and Tommie and it was too late to ask him what he meant. He was back on the surface of insincerity again.

"You two guys alright?" Willie asked.

"Shit, yeah," Tommie answered. "What about you two?"

Willie slapped the dashboard.

"There's nothing wrong here that a tune-up won't fix."

"Huh?" Tommie wheezed. He looked at French in the hope of clearing up his bewilderment.

French pointed at his own right ear and vigorously spun his finger around it in a small circle to indicate that Willie was crazy.

"Are you two clowns going to stand out there all night or do you want a ride home?" Willie complained.

"Home! The night is still young," Tommie boasted incredulously.

"Yeah, well. . .let's see if the girls are still there. It's no fun without the girls, now."

"Damn it all, Willie. You planned to do this tonight," Tommie said in a sudden fit of revelation.

"I plan nothing," Willie said harshly.

"Maybe that's your problem," French countered in Tommie's defense.

"Maybe. Then I would end up like you."

I didn't like the tone or the direction this conversation was taking.

"Jesus Christ, shut up! We're acting like a bunch of kids," I finally said before French's resentment took any shape.

My statement succeeded in silencing everyone. That was good enough for me. I had gained control of a bad situation, somehow. Even though control was the very thing I did not want.

      wrong
      not because I was so very right
      . . .because I displayed anger

Chapter 24
Intermezzo

He was an Apache Indian and he was drunk. I watched him throw himself off the top landing of a flight of stairs. He had lost his nerve and didn't want to go out on another patrol. He didn't want to die. All he wanted to do was break his legs and get medevaced home. But he was drunk, too drunk to break anything. I know. I watched him throw himself off the top landing of that flight of stairs three more times.

He was too drunk to hurt himself and he gave up trying. I encouraged him to stop. I did not know he had given up hope. I was drunk, too. Two days later, he was dead. Killed in action. I didn't see him die.

Another chink of light in my memory; another assault by man-made shadows.

> everything recedes into the past
> everything except the memory of war
>
> torn a little each day and
> nights are filled with sounds:
> small arms fire and the cries of men
> I once knew; now realizing these boys
>
> were playing on a killing ground, dressed
> with the illusion of immortality

*   *   *   *

We always got lost within the demands of academic life during the school year at Florida State. Catherine and I were devoted students. But occasionally, when the pressure became intolerable, we managed to convince ourselves to throw an afternoon away by packing a lunch and driving out to McClay Gardens.

Our humble lunch would consist of peanut butter sandwiches supported by a thermos of black coffee. The implements of our entertainment were equally humble and consisted of a blanket spread out under a canopy made of trees that stood a comfortable distance away from the narrow trail which led to that vicinity.

To say "a canopy made of trees" is almost misleading because one may imagine a single clump of trees standing in isolation off a trail. This is not the case at McClay Gardens, which is a refuge for trees and for a well-tended botanical garden. So, to walk any distance away from the gardens means to encounter a sky filled with Spanish moss and intermittent towering pines.

Entertainment itself was a commune with nature: resting, gazing, dozing—actively doing nothing even if that meant slapping a mosquito or brushing away an ant. Bird sounds filled us up and squirrels scampering in and around trees carried us away; all urban perspectives in what was essentially a controlled environment.

Remember, our lives were quite artificial: classrooms and libraries and study lounges; then home to eat, study, and sleep—all our time predominantly inside man-made structures. So, the contrast of McClay Gardens was heavenly. I knew this; therefore, I was in heaven. I knew this; therefore, I was in love.

> speed limit:
> 10 m.p.h.
> warning:
> Beware of Dog
>
> rural declarations
> posted civilization
>
> standing
> along a dirt road

Chapter 25
Milk and Cereal

The next morning I managed to get up before everyone else. It was a few minutes before eight o'clock on a Saturday morning. I had to remind myself that I had to meet Ted at the donut stop by ten.

I was moderately hung over and wanted some milk with cold cereal for breakfast. I quietly slipped out of the house, after choking down a couple of aspirins, and walked several blocks to the grocery store. The sun had not burned through the relative cool morning sky and the humidity was not too uncomfortable yet. This was unusual. And I was thankful. I had to hurry.

I quickly forgot my timetable once I was greeted by the supermarket's air conditioning. Eventually, I found myself standing in the middle of the supermarket's aisle in front of a three-tiered row of cereal boxes trying to decide which box I wanted to go along with the container of milk I was holding in my right hand. I was completely lost within the maze of colors and brand names when I gently staggered to my right a couple of steps. I was about to excuse myself, thinking it was an accidental collision by someone passing by, when it happened again. This was deliberate. My morning passivity quickly transformed into anger at the two figures planted before me.

"He's the guy," said the shorter one of the two.

"I'm the guy, what?" I glared in response.

"You want me to take him?" the taller one said as if I weren't there.

The shorter one responded by approaching me with the intent to shove me aside once again. His face registered surprise when I parried his attempt and followed through with a push that forced him to crash into the grocery shelves stocked with boxes of corn flakes.

I no longer felt the chill of the supermarket air conditioning. The heat of battle was beginning to boil within me. By the time the shorter fellow righted and repositioned himself squarely before me, I decided I didn't care to find out who these guys were or what their reason was for their attack. I placed the container of milk on the floor. Then I gingerly clenched my fists and raised them to a waist high level in a cavalier display of readiness.

He hesitated. He began to lose confidence. The engagement of this "two against one" tactic was not working out. He was a coward.

"What are you waiting for?" he snarled.

I said nothing. The taller one circled to the left several steps before he spoke.

"I think you've got yourself something here, Drew. You want me to take him?"

Haughtiness got the best of cowardice during a hesitant interval of tight-lipped silence by the shorter one called Drew.

"I can take him," he said. He raised his fists chest high. "Come on, let's do it."

"No," I finally said. "Let's go outside, out back, where nobody can stop us before we're finished."

The taller one whistled aloud in a breathy exhale.

"Boy, you've got a live one there, Drew."

Drew faltered for another moment before he finally countered my challenge.

"Come on, right here. What are you afraid of?"

The measured smile that cracked from my mouth startled him. His dark eyes shifted uneasily. He licked his lips. His friend was astute enough to know the fight was already lost.

"Back away, Drew."

"I'll handle this, Mark!" Drew snapped irritably.

The fingers of his clenched fist tightened and relaxed several times before he settled on an opposing stance that he was satisfied with. I knew his palms were sweaty. I knew he couldn't take a punch. I knew the belly underneath his tee shirt was soft. I knew his knock-knees would buckle with my first blow. I knew that his carefully constructed nose would break easily. He was a bully, a coward, completely out of his element now that he was facing someone who was not afraid of him. He needed a good beating and

I was just the person to give it to him. To his amazement, I swaggered past him in a way that communicated my intention. He had no alternative but to follow me outside.

The usual wall of Florida humidity assaulted me and raised the level of my body heat into an immediate sweat which soaked through the front of my tee shirt. I didn't stop to wait for my enemy. Instead, I proceeded to my right and circled around the building until I reached the back lot near a dumpster. I could feel an intense but silent chatter transpiring between my two opponents as they followed me. And as soon as I was satisfied with the privacy of the location, I turned to them and raised my clenched fists in readiness to fight. I said two words.

"Let's go."

The taller one broke away from the shorter one in a quiet resolve that betrayed his determination not to interfere; no matter what the final outcome. I had already cleanly succeeded in dividing the enemy; the messy business of conquering was all that was left.

I struck the first blow as I recalled my childhood instructions from my father. "There is no honor in waiting for the first blow. Hit your opponent first. Knock the wind out of his sails. Then hit him again. Most fights are won, or decided, by these two blows."

My right fist connected to his face just below his left eye. It shattered his grim countenance into a putty-like expression. His body bent slightly backward and to the right in response. Before he could recover, I came around with a left hook into the softness of his belly. This forced an intense groan to accompany the exhale that brought him to his knees. He gasped for breath as he clutched his belly with both hands. It was over. Easily. Completely. I turned my attention toward the other coward. He raised his hands high into the air as if a western six-shooter was pointed into his back.

"Hey, it's not my fight. I didn't start anything. Frances is his woman, not mine."

Now I understood the reason for this fight and the extent of their cowardice.

"Frances is not his woman," I said decisively. And then, maliciously, for the first time in my life, I walked over to a man, this Drew who was still on his knees gasping for air, and grabbed him by the hair. I twisted his agonized face toward mine until we were almost nose to nose.

"And if you ever lay a hand on her again," I said, "I'll break both of your arms."

The sight of him disgusted me, and I succumbed to an evil temptation by throwing his face into the ground rather than simply releasing my grip. A tiny pang of regret winced through me when I heard the impact against the cement of the back lot. Then I looked at the taller one called Mark.

"Don't ever challenge me again."

He remained silent. His face flushed red, accenting his freckles and his carrot-colored hair.

I turned away and sauntered back around to the front of the supermarket. I involuntarily began to shake all over once I was sure I was out of their sight. It was leftover rage and the realization that I had faced death. That's why I won. I was willing to face death. I always died before death and therefore lived. Vietnam had given me that in its crudest form. But it was Jansen, yes, Jansen who had brought this complex notion of the undead, the unborn, to its present refinement. "Give no thought to losing and you will win; give no thought to death and you will live." Those had been Jansen's words. His thoughts. No-thoughts. My thoughts. The result of my thoughts.

I went back into the supermarket and bought my milk and cereal. I was no longer hung over.

Chapter 26
Too Miserable to Think

I got back to the house in plenty of time to eat a couple of bowls of cereal and gulp down a cup of coffee. A quick rinse under the shower invigorated me and woke Frances up. She stumbled into the hallway as I was coming out of the bathroom. She looked terribly hung over. On one side, her hair was flat against her head.

"There's milk and cereal in the refrigerator," I said to her.

"Yuk, sounds terrible," she said as she pulled the belt of French's bathrobe a little tighter around her waist. "How can you eat? What time is it?"

"About nine-thirty," I said.

"Is there any coffee?"

"Sure," I said. "But you're going to have to make it. I've got to go to work."

"I've got to have a cigarette."

A sudden pang of queasiness made her reach for her stomach. She gently rubbed it with her hand.

"Are you going to be alright?"

"Yeah. I'm just hung over."

"There's aspirin in the medicine cabinet."

"Right."

"Gotta go."

"How can you go to work after last night?"

"It hurts more if I don't."

Frances almost smiled. "Go on. Get out of here. I'm going back to bed."

Chapter 27
"There's no hope."

I was there all day.
Not half there. Not half doing.
The pain of the sun was mine.
And so was the joy.
Sweat poured from my forehead,
soaked my eyebrows and burned my eyes;
I forgot my hat!
But I owned my pain. I was free!
I had no hope. No need for anything else.
Everything was perfectly real:
     the lawn mower perfectly loud,
     the sun perfectly hot,
     the grass perfectly green.
This was my reward. Nothing at all.
There was no secret to the truth.

I drove the riding mower over to Ted after I finished the last narrow strip of grass and turned off the motor. The right corner of his mouth was projected slightly upward in a half smile. He was carefully studying my face.

"What in the world are you so happy about?" he asked.

"Me?" I said. "Nothing."

He looked at me suspiciously.

"You better not be smoking any of that wacky weed."

I chuckled at him and stepped off the mower.

"I'm thirsty. Have we got anything in the cooler?"

"There's a couple of drinks left. Let's get everything into the trailer before we take a break."

After we had finished packing up, he dug out two drinks from the ice chest and handed me one. I drank my soda until the carbonation burned the back of my throat. I had to stop drinking.

"Boy that tastes good," I said.

"You're a hard worker. Here." He handed me my pay. "I don't work on Sundays. Can you start early Monday morning?"

"What time?"

"Seven."

"Sure."

"Donut shop alright?"

"Why not?"

"Good." He shook his head.

"What," I said.

"Someday."

"What?"

"Someday you're not going to show up."

"So?"

"So, I'm going to have to keep reminding myself of that."

This was as good a compliment about my work as I could ever expect from a man like Ted. I looked out over the freshly cut lawn.

"This is the best that I can do for you, Ted. There's no hope."

He stepped alongside me to admire the finished job.

"I'm an ordinary guy, Mr. Llewellen. Hope is all I got."

I wanted to tell him that there was no use hoping that somewhere there had to be more than this. That there was nothing wrong with dreams as long as he didn't hold onto them. The constant flow of air, the mental-torpor state that went with riding for hours on a lawn mower was all there was. His standing beside me smelling the fresh-cut grass was all there was. Our breaths, our bodies, our surroundings, now. . .was all there was of eternity. There was no hope for anything else. No past. No future. No present. Only this, just this; our very life, here. . .was paradise.

I looked at Ted. The bulge in his cheek filled with chewing tobacco was as prominent as ever. I wanted to ask him, where did he think we were? Where was his paradise lost? But I chose my own brand of alienation rather than accept his. A glob of brown liquid spewed from his mouth and landed several feet away from us.

"You want to try some?" he winked proudly.

"No thanks," I said without revealing my distaste.

We continued to drink our sodas and enjoy the smell of fresh-cut grass.

gazing with weightless thoughts
into the heat of the day
presence. . .no presence. . .

Chapter 28
"I didn't do anything."

Frances jumped up to greet me. She had been sitting on the living room sofa talking to Janet.

"Janet helped me find a job as a waitress today. It's part-time," Frances said. "I start tomorrow."

"How did you manage that with your hangover?" I asked.

"The same way you went to work this morning. I can't let you pay for everything." Her attitude became solemn. "And I don't want to take advantage of French."

My contact with the coolness of central air conditioning had sent a chill through my body. Perspiration had completely soaked through my tee shirt and had bled halfway down my blue jeans to my pockets. The money I had folded into my right front pocket felt damp. I smiled.

"There's nothing wrong with that," I said to Frances as I studied Janet.

She was a beautiful woman. And her generosity at giving Frances the attention she needed made me appreciate the fullness of her inner comeliness.

"Thanks, Janet," I said.

"I didn't do anything. Just took the car and drove Fran around to a few places. She found the job."

Janet had long, soft, straight, golden brown hair that fell to her waist. Her lovely eyes were large and dark brown. But their gentleness had been replaced with a brand of bitterness caused by a constant domestic squabbling between her and Willie. This produced a worn-out demeanor which slightly blemished the incredible beauty of her delicate facial features. Even a smile could not hide the general state of her unhappiness.

The warm glow of her skin and her perfect complexion gave an overall impression of good health. Her figure was petite, her manner was graceful and her femininity was natural. She stood four feet eleven inches high in sneakers, jeans, and a tee shirt. But her well-proportioned figure improved the ordinary appearance of this uniform.

"Thanks, anyway," I insisted.

"You want a beer?" Frances asked.

"I want a bath. Too tired for a beer," I said.

I shuffled toward the hallway as I peeled off my wet tee shirt. I wondered how Frances managed to explain or conceal from her employer the bandage wrapped around her wrist. I didn't ask.

"Wait," Frances said.

"What?" I responded.

"You haven't heard the real news, yet."

"And?"

Frances looked at Janet as if waiting for her permission to go on. Janet nodded, yes.

"Janet is moving in with us."

"I'm leaving Willie," Janet hastened to qualify. She was a little nervous, even apprehensive.

"You don't have to give me any reasons, Janet. If there's anything I can do, just let me know."

She became calm again.

"I'm staying with French."

I hesitated. "I see."

"No you don't."

A silence spread between us.

"So, what's new," I responded.

Chapter 29
Associations

A week and a half went by, and, with the passage of that time, a household routine of work, play, and sleep had been established. Janet did not seem worried that Willie had disappeared without a trace. In fact, she would not talk about it. And whatever was happening between French and Janet remained a mystery. In spite of the morning's bathroom congestion and the general over-crowded living conditions, we managed to get along quite well.

It was late for a work night. Everyone else was asleep. I sat quietly at the kitchen table with a pen poised over a blank sheet of paper for a long time. I didn't know what to say, so I removed Zack's recent letter to me from its envelope.

Dear Llew,
What is alone? The most important koan of all. It follows you into birth; it leads the way toward death.
So, what is the problem? You're still searching. Life and death. That's the whole relationship. You have to know what it means to look. Whatever you see is an association: this letter you are holding, the words you are reading, the chair you are probably sitting on. . .associations (not just with people). There's nothing more. What do you want? What else is there to being alone?

There are no answers
if there are no questions.
You don't have to count your breaths,
you don't have to do anything
when you sit.

Zack

P.S. You once mentioned that your family lived in Miami. So, I went to the public library. There was only one Llewellen spelled in this manner in the Miami telephone book.

I laid Zack's letter on the table, picked up my pen, and began to write.

Dear Zack,
I'm cutting grass for a living. At times, the sun becomes so hot, the grass is cutting me. Do I know what practice is? Or am I just talking. Do I know how to live zazen after I finish sitting? Or am I just fitting all this into another compartment in my life?

I still have questions.
Why must I confuse myself
with more answers?
Llew

Chapter 30
"Hurry," she whispered.

I woke up from a dead sleep. It was dark and my eyes strained for every ray of light. I turned my head and read 3 a.m. on the face of the alarm clock.

Frances was asleep beside me, or so I thought. I listened for her shallow breath of slumber, but it was not there. When I rolled over onto my left side to listen more closely, she entwined herself against me in one swift gentle movement. She punctuated her intention with the softest kiss I had ever experienced. I became aroused. She became aroused; then afraid. I waited. Her intention became unclear to me. Neither of us spoke. Instead, we allowed ourselves to become accustomed to the warmth of our body contact. It was a warmth that could only be generated by actual skin contact: I was not wearing a shirt and the light cotton night gown she borrowed from Janet had slipped all the way up to her chest.

This was as close as we had come to making love. She wrapped her legs into mine. Skin contact. Sexual trembling between us. My caution. Her reluctance. Our growing intimacy, pushing and pulling without force. But our desire did not overcome the tangible fear she had derived from some past violation; we held ourselves in check.

She kissed me again. This time I responded just as tenderly. I ached for her. I wanted to slip her panties off but I restrained myself. She pulled them down herself.

"Hurry," she whispered.

She gently tugged at my shorts. I pulled away from her.

"I'm sorry," I uttered. "I can't."

She became still, not tense; quiet, not silent. I rolled onto my back. When she laid her head on my chest, I felt the wetness of her tears. A long time passed before she spoke.

"You're as screwed up as I am," she said.

"That should make us friends."

She raised her head off of my chest. Her eyes pierced through the darkness between us. "We're going to fail, you know."

"Is that how you see everything?" I asked.

"It's the truth," she stated coldly. "And I'm afraid of the truth."

The silence that followed prevailed until the stillness between us gave way to an uneasy slumber.

Chapter 31
Intermezzo

Between patrols we all smoked too much marijuana. But consumption was not limited to this substance for a high. Marijuana was simply our staple high that was constantly fortified with liquid speed, barbiturates, opium, cocaine, amphetamines, and anything else we could get our hands on. Of course, beer was always available. But LSD and hashish were virtually impossible to get unless somebody had it mailed in from the states.

The amount of our consumption was staggering. It was probably proportional to the stress of mortal danger we faced each day. For most of us, it provided a method of escape until we met our death or were sent home. Tragically, death and being sent home became synonymous in my unit. To have survived was the exception, not the rule. I survived.

I would not feel guilty. I was a majority. I deserved my life.

> constantly pulled by demands:
> people and their practicalities
> people wanting to update your taste
> rather than improve their own
>
> absolutely necessary, their
> need to manipulate one into position
>
> the majority of one: me
> constantly not fitting in
> the majority of one: me
> dangerously exploring the truth
>
> absolutely unnecessary, this
> verse is what's left in the end

*　　*　　*　　*

Catherine and I rarely went to parties but, when we did, we usually paid the price of heavy hangovers and much regret. The cause of our hangovers was alcohol. But the source of our regret was a basic insecurity with people. Especially after long exposure to them. Fortunately, we had each other to reconstruct our self-esteem to a serviceable level the following morning.

God, I loved that woman. She was me and I was her. I could not imagine myself without those years with her. I would not have survived the war without her.

Dead, all dead; while I survive.

> You either believe in God
> or you don't.
>
> I believe in God
> but there is no God.
> Where does that leave existence
> or non existence?
>
> Life is a dream
> but you also die.
> And if you have a funeral
> people will have to pray.
>
> So, why is life
> so sad?

Chapter 32
"Where is the meaning?"

Another day had blended into another night. Ted and I had worked until the approach of twilight. He paid me, as usual, in front of the donut shop where he left me. I was tired. I did not want to go home. I had no plans.

I walked around to the side of the building to get away from the noise of the traffic and bury myself into the relative comfort of darkness, deepened by the cast of the building's shadow. I took off my bamboo hat and wiped the sweat off my forehead with the back of my forearm.

"The night is blue."

I turned to the voice. Willie appeared. He was drunk; miserable; beyond sympathy.

"Then it's no longer a color," I said.

"So?"

"You're the one who cares."

Willie took a hard drink from a pint bottle he was holding. I looked around for his car but I couldn't see it.

"I love her, Llew."

"But you hate yourself."

"That's right." Willie laughed. "You're too smart, Llew. How come you don't have anything?" I didn't answer him. He took a deep breath, then exhaled miserably. "It's closing in on me, man."

"What?"

"The world. Haven't you heard? It all comes to an end." He finished the bottle and pitched it into the night. The sound of glass splashed when it hit the cement. "I won't go back, Llew."

"I don't know what to tell you, Will. . .except, it isn't so bad. I was there before you, remember?"

"Yeah, and look at you," he laughed.

"The Marine Corps. . .the War. . .had nothing to do with what I am now." I grimaced. "You're soft, Willie. You're spoiled. I can't help you."

"Because you can't help yourself," Willie finished.

"I'm not afraid of the truth, man."

"When you see it, make sure you keep it a secret. I want to die misunderstood."

"Where are you going, Willie?"

"To hell."

"There's no such place."

"Then there's no place."

"That's right."

"I knew you were crazy."

Willie pulled out a revolver,

"Don't do it, Will."

"You're reading between the lines, Llew."

"I won't judge you."

"But you do see things as they are. Damn you. Look at me!"

Willie pointed the revolver to his head. He peered at me while frozen in that position.

"Aren't you going to do something?"

"That won't stop you," I answered.

Willie lowered the gun.

"I can't kill myself in front of you. It feels like a sin. And. . .I'm a coward. I can't live with myself."

"Janet loves you."

Willie sneered.

"Janet doesn't love herself, either."

He pivoted the revolver with his forefinger, then spun himself completely around one time in a display of sheer madness.

"What happened, Llew? What happened to the answers we were going to find? Where is the meaning? Where?"

"I can't give you words. I'm sorry."

"Some help you are."

Willie started to walk away again.

"Wait. Don't go," I said.

But Willie disappeared around the rear corner of the building without answering me. Without giving me another chance to fail him. I felt sick inside.

How could I show him that life was great? That there was no

mystery. That it didn't matter. That words. . .

I had to try words one last time. I shouted into the direction of his disappearance.

"I'd rather be alone than dead!"

I stepped out of the dark cast of the building's shade to emphasize my words; I created my own shadow, instead. It began to rain.

I put my hat back on, turned around, and started walking in the opposite direction with no destination in mind; with no mind at all. . .

> shadows
> a reflection
> of silence; visible
> when looking beyond one's empty
> extremes

Chapter 33
"Don't embarrass me, Llew."

I had not taken a bath yet.

I had not told Janet about Will.

I still hadn't paid French a penny.

French, Tommie, and Janet were in the living room watching television. I raised my hand in a hollow wave and shuffled across the room and down the hallway. I found myself standing in the middle of the bedroom listening to Frances.

"I simply have to have my purse," Frances stated irritably. "I've got no identification. The restaurant wants to see my social security card. What am I going to do?"

"Nothing. I'll get your purse for you," I said.

Her eyes widened with shock.

"No, Llew, I was just blowing off steam. You don't know Drew."

"Yes, I do."

"The landlord, Mr. Sanchez, will let me into the house. He'll understand."

I followed her into the kitchen. She was excited; even glowing with anticipation. She opened one of the kitchen drawers and pulled out a folded shopping bag. I suddenly grabbed her by the arm. It was an impulse. Involuntary. Not angry; suspicious. I did not like the level of her enthusiasm.

"Tell me you're not one of those."

"Let go of my arm."

I let go. "Sorry." She smacked the drawer shut.

"Men." She rattled the shopping bag at my face. "I want some of my things, that's all! The violence you suspect me of liking is within you." With determination. "I'm going to get my stuff right now."

"I'm coming."

"I don't want your help," she said firmly.

I looked at Frances. It was useless for me to say again that I was sorry. I walked over to the same drawer where she had found the bag and removed one for myself. I unfolded it and placed it over my head. It put an end to Fran's mounting tirade.

"Don't embarrass me, Llew."

"I have wiped all expression from my face."

"Only one of them made me angry."

"I'm not taking any chances."

She snickered.

"You're goofy. But I like you."

I pulled the bag off of my head. Her expression became serious once again.

"Don't ever think bad of me, Llew."

"I won't."

"I don't like where I've been," she said. "He used to beat me. I won't let that happen to me again."

"If he shows up while we're there, it could get ugly," I said.

"I won't be afraid of him," she said with determination. "I no longer have a limp. And see? The bruise on my arm is almost gone."

"Okay," I said. But I was concerned. Alone, I was one on one with Drew; I had control. Having Frances with me would change that. I still wasn't sure how she would react.

"I can handle this, Llew."

"Okay," I said.

Chapter 34
Delicious!

We traveled west on Coral Way until we reached 107th Avenue, where we made a left turn. Tommie, French, and Janet had overheard my argument with Frances and had insisted on coming with us. The two-car parade then proceeded toward the Westwood Lake area.

Drew and Frances had lived together in a rented house under the strain of a painful relationship. I couldn't understand why Fran would allow herself to be hurt and manipulated in such a gross fashion.

How many layers of self-deceit and delusion were required to live in such a manner? I thought. What were her dreams? And why were her attachments for them so strong? What made them so important? To think, she was willing to kill herself rather than live without them. The structure of all these layers were more important than the actual structure of herself. She was killing that self daily. She was lost in her fantasies while her true life was going by unnoticed.

Her tragedy moved me. It made me think about the Zen parable Jansen once told me.

I closed my eyes and envisioned the man who was being chased by a tiger. The man finally reached a point where there was nothing left for him to do but jump off a cliff in order to escape. And on his way down he managed to grab onto a vine and prolong his life. As the lion pawed at him from above, he looked below and saw another lion waiting for him to fall. To make matters worse, a couple of mice scampered onto the vine, his life line, and began gnawing on it. Suddenly, he caught sight of a beautiful ripe strawberry. He reached over with one hand, plucked the strawberry, and ate it. Delicious!

"Life is a tragedy," Jansen said.

I was no longer in the car with Tommie and Frances. I was in a dream, in a memory, with Chris and Jansen; the past was now the present. We were in a car and we had just pulled away from my ex-girlfriend Lydia, who had wanted to come with us. Chris was driving. Jansen was hurt. I was worried. At the time, I didn't know Jansen was dying. He had received the fatal blow from Barbara's jealous fiancée, Pete. I sat in the back seat with Jansen, looking through the rearview mirror at Pete. He was in the street, dancing with anger beside Lydia's forlorn figure. He was still brandishing the revolver he had threatened to use against Jansen.

"I thought you said that everything in life is okay, as it is," I said.

"In life, yes; in your life, no," Jansen said.

"I see what I see."

"Delusions. Pain. Right and Wrong. Good and evil. You've learned nothing. We're dead from the beginning. Why do you spend your life in a pointless battle to evade that end? That's tragedy. And it's okay. The strawberry should taste as good one minute from your death as it would near your birth."

"Why didn't you fight back, Jan?" I pounced at him vehemently.

"I did, Llew," he said innocently.

"Damn that Pete. You could have been killed the way he struck you."

Jansen winced with pain.

"But I am dead. And alive," he said.

I was bewildered. And I was worried by the white pallor of his face.

"There's no such thing," I contested.

"That's right. Isn't every moment of our life the last thing, the last moment? There's no moment other than this." The perplexity clouding my eyes amused Jansen. "Poor, Llewellen. Sure we die. But if the strawberry tastes good just a second before that, then where is the problem? See? Tragedy from your point of view. No tragedy from life's point of view."

I became angry in the way a mother gets angry with a child who has foolishly done something dangerous and has narrowly escaped from harm.

"You could have fought back," I said.

"I did. And so did you. Nobody said not to. But in the end, whatever the end, it's okay. No problem. Delicious."

Jansen shuddered through another episode of pain. I shifted myself toward the end of the seat as Jansen curled up into a ball and slid onto his side.

"Maybe we should go to a hospital," I said.

"No hospitals, Llew. I'll be all right. Just let me lie here a minute."

I was worried. When I looked down at Jansen's face, I saw he was smiling up at me.

"Poor Llewellen. You are miserable."

"I am."

"You are worried."

"I am."

"Then just be that."

"What?"

"The absolute truth. Stop listening."

I couldn't understand. So I directed him to the problems of myself in the present.

"What would you do in this situation, Jan? Shall I stop Drew from hurting Fran?"

"Of course. Haven't I already shown you?"

"But you didn't do anything."

"But you weren't looking. See? I got hurt."

My forehead crinkled, reflecting my great mental effort.

"I can't think, Jan."

"The problem is you do."

"I don't know what to do."

"It's done. You hit Barbara's boyfriend, Pete."

"No, I mean about Drew and Frances."

"That's what I said. It's the same thing."

"It's not the same thing, Jan."

"Oh. That's right. It's no-thing at all."

"You drive me crazy."

Jansen laughed. Or was it I hearing Jansen's laughter which was my own laughter as I experienced the dream of these kaleidoscope recollections; which brought me back to the present by inviting Tommie to intrude upon my thoughts. I opened my eyes.

"You must have nerves of steel, Llew," Tommie said, keeping his eyes on the road as he drove.

My trance finally dissipated.

111

"What do you mean, Tom?"

"How can you laugh?" he asked.

Frances looked at me expectantly but she remained quiet.

"Delicious," I mumbled unintelligibly to myself. I turned around to see if French and Janet were still following close behind us. They were. "When we get there, Tom, make sure French and Janet stay in their car."

"Okay."

"Take a left on the next block," Frances directed.

"Right," Tommie said.

"Fran and I are going in alone."

Tommie began to protest but I quickly prevented him from doing so.

"I want you out here to keep an eye on things. Above all, keep French and Janet out of this. If Drew and that sidekick of his— what's his name?"

"Mark," Frances quickly answered.

"If Drew and this Mark show up," I continued, "then follow them into the house. I'll need your help then."

"Alright," Tommie said. He looked at Frances. "I don't want her getting hurt."

"Agreed," I said.

Frances seemed to melt into the seat between us.

"Who needs a social security card, anyway," she tried to say offhandedly in order to convince us that this confrontation was not necessary.

"Sorry, Fran," Tommie said, "the decision is made."

"But. . . ," Frances looked at Tommie long and hard and knew that it would be pointless to protest. She didn't even bother to turn around and look at me. She punctuated the silence by striking a match which highlighted the darkness with the tiny blaze of fire she used to touch the end of a cigarette. The tone of her voice was a bit hollow when she finally spoke.

"Make a right turn at the corner. It's the third house on the left."

Chapter 35
Judgments

The house was a single-story, white stucco structure. Frances was pointing out that the landlord lived in the next house as we approached the main entrance. But I motioned her into silence. I took out my laminated driver's license and walked up to the front door. I cautiously turned around to make sure the street was clear before inserting the license through the crack near the lock where the door latch met the doorjamb.

Our two automobiles were parked across the street and several houses down. Tommie had joined French and Janet in the second car. Together, the three of them blended into the darkness of the unlit street and further into the darkness of the automobile's interior.

The license easily slipped past the latch, and with a quick jiggle the door was open. I stepped into the darkness with Frances close behind me.

There was no air conditioning. I immediately began to perspire. The smell of mildew and the thickness of the humidity almost suffocated me. I had to turn on a light or go mad.

One word described my first impression the instant the overhead light flooded the living room: squalor. The discomfort I felt in the darkness had increased with lightness. The smell of rotten garbage strangled me; my tee shirt was now completely soaked with sweat.

"You lived like this?" I finally said to Frances.

"Of course not," she said.

She was almost as offended by my remark as she was by our surroundings. She peered at all corners of the room with distaste, fear, and urgency.

"Hurry up and pack," I said. "We don't have all night. What can I do to help?"

"Just stay where you are. I won't take but a minute." She disappeared down a hall toward the bedrooms.

It was impossible not to judge Drew and even Frances. I knew I was separating myself from the world with this dualistic thinking. It was hard to believe that everything here was perfect, as it was, perfectly filthy; piles of roach-infested garbage stacked up behind the sofa against the living room wall and beside mounds of dirty clothes. I felt uneasy, even repulsed by the stench. Beer cans, layers of leftover food and even broken glass littered the floor. I had to remind myself what Jansen once said to me: "There are no such things as evil forces; there are only evil acts. This is different. Oppose evil acts, not people. Otherwise we judge, we become righteous, and we condemn everyone; even ourselves."

I knew Jansen's line of reasoning brought me right back to what Jansen called our essential nature: no-thing. Jansen believed that man had the ability to live beyond good and evil; that man would simply act in accordance with nature if dualistic thinking were stripped away. Jansen left me confused. I wish he were alive to clarify this point. I was beginning to get frustrated and I was beginning to get a headache. I wished I could sit in zazen right now and stop thinking. I did the next best thing.

"Why does Drew beat you?" I called out to Frances.

She returned to the living room with a large white canvas handbag in one hand and the shopping bag in the other. They were bulging with the personal items she had hastily packed into them.

"I don't know. He gets angry." She thought for a moment. "Maybe it's because I can't have a baby."

"That's ridiculous," I said.

"He's ridiculous. He's crazy. I don't know." She approached me and placed her belongings on the floor. "Anyway, something good came out of it. We didn't get married."

I looked at the two bundles.

"Is that everything?" I asked.

"It's all I've got to show for my life. Pitiful, isn't it?"

There it was, I thought. Judgments.

"Pitiful is a word," I finally said.

"But the right one," a voice from behind added with a snarl.

I turned around and discovered Drew and Mark standing at the open doorway. They entered but kept their distance. I could see that Drew was reluctant to get within my reach. But his apparent fear of me did not dampen his impudence.

"What are you two doing here?" Drew demanded.

Mark circled around to my right. I didn't move. Mark also kept his distance. They were both wary of my ability to strike. Frances defensively hurled her words at Drew.

"I'm getting my stuff."

"Look at this bitch, Mark. She's all ready to scurry out of here with two bags full of shit."

"It's my shit," she countered with equal venom.

"Everything in here, including you, is mine," Drew declared.

"This place stinks," she said.

"So do you, bitch."

Drew circled around me. He began strutting toward her as soon as he was past me. I shifted my position in order to keep an eye on both of them. Mark was now to my left and Drew was to my right facing Frances. She had maintained her defiant position.

I noticed that Drew's carefully constructed nose was slightly out of joint as a result of our fight at the supermarket. The tee shirt tucked into his trousers did not conceal the slight bulge of his soft belly protruding over his belt. He seemed even more squat because of the excessive deformity of his knock-knees. I couldn't help myself. Judgments. I disliked the man immensely. He was physically a slob and mentally a coward. I decided to let him play his game.

"Why don't you give up and admit it to yourself. You missed me," Drew said to Frances.

"Like a cup of hemlock," she spat.

"You came back to papa and papa will give you what you like most." Drew gyrated his hips a couple of times to emphasize the bulge between his legs.

Mark laughed at the crude sexual innuendo. He had broken teeth. I hadn't noticed that before. It made him appear more satanic when he laughed or grinned. He had very short red hair, almost a crew cut, and very long sideburns from another time. He wore a short-sleeved shirt that only partially concealed a set of large tattoos which covered both his upper arms. He was tall but not very big. He was mostly legs. Mark finally spoke.

"Shove your dick into her, man. That'll straighten her out."

How could Frances have been a part of this? I wondered. Who was she?

I looked at her. It was hard not to judge.

"Hey, bud." Drew was speaking to me. "You don't want this skinny, flat-chested bitch, do you? Just look at her." His voice was contemptuous. It effectively made Frances shrink before my eyes. Whatever measure of self-confidence she had completely dissolved. "I could make her fuck all three of us. You want me to show you how?"

"No," I finally said, having heard enough. "But I'm going to show you how I'm going to bust this up."

My threat placed us all on guard. Drew pulled out a large pocket knife and opened it. The blade was large and sharp.

"I'm going to kill you," he said as he turned away from Frances. She was thoroughly frightened. She knew he meant what he said.

"Watch him, Llew, he'll do it," Frances warned nervously.

But even though Drew was now armed, he remained wary. His leeriness infected Mark. And just when I was beginning to wonder where Tommie was, I heard his voice.

"I saw these two come up here and I thought you could use my help."

Drew was noticeably shaken by the turn of events. He growled in an attempt to conceal his uneasiness.

"So, you brought help with you," Drew said.

"I don't need help against you two," I said.

"Mark's going to take you apart," Drew said.

"Like you tried to do at the supermarket?" I said.

"What supermarket?" Frances asked.

"Don't get smart, buddy," Mark declared.

"On second thought, I can use your help, Tom. Would you get French and Janet to drive Fran home?"

"Sure," Tommie said.

"And help her take her things to the car," I instructed.

"You want me to stay around afterwards?" Tommie asked.

"Of course," I said. "I need a ride home."

My bluff was working and both Drew and Mark were wilting on the vine. I looked at Mark; my eyes pierced his. I knew that the present showdown was with him this time. Drew was the basic kind of coward that didn't want another beating from me. I felt my eyes penetrate into Mark's core. His countenance changed; became softer.

Zen doesn't mean inaction, I thought. I also remembered that it doesn't mean cruelty, either. I would react, not act; do, not undo.

Mark relaxed his stance to match his softer countenance.

"I don't like this, Drew." Mark began to sway a bit.

Drew knew he had to act quickly, if they were to save face.

"Christ, you're right," Drew agreed as he circled back around me toward Mark. "They've got people outside waiting for them. You heard him. There are too many witnesses for. . ." Drew waved his knife, then slashed the air a couple of times to display what he had intended to do.

Mark brightened suddenly. He saw their loophole of escape. He was no less a coward.

"You're right. Let's get out of here."

"No," Drew snarled. "Let them get out of here. It's my place." He almost sounded like a child demanding his ball because he was losing the game. "Get out of here. All of you."

"You hear that, Tom?" I said.

"The man says, get out," Tommie snickered.

"After you, Frances," I said.

"And you," Drew hissed as he pointed at her. "You'll be back. And when you do, it's going to be worse on you."

"Go to hell," I finally said.

"Yeah," Drew countered. "But I'm going to kill you first."

I tossed one of Fran's bag's to Tommie and carried the canvas one myself.

"See what I mean, Frances?" I said as I escorted her out of the house. "Words, nothing but words."

I couldn't help myself. I knew the sound of my sarcasm was dangerous at this point. But fortunately everyone else was smart enough to remain silent, now that the outcome of the game had been decided. Drew and Mark were careful not to make any quick or decisive moves as the three of us passed through their gauntlet on our way out of the front door. As soon as the door closed behind us, we scurried through the darkness toward the two vehicles.

"What happened?" French whispered.

"Don't ask," I said. "Let's get the hell out of here."

French drove off with Janet. And Tommie had his car started by the time I hopped in beside Frances. I placed the white canvas bag I was carrying on her lap.

"Jesus Christ," Tommie said, as he pulled the gearshift into drive and stepped on the gas. "Who were those guys?"

I couldn't say. I wouldn't. To judge them was to judge Frances. I kept silent to keep from making judgments upon myself. I turned around as Frances lit a cigarette and looked through the rearview window.

Chapter 36
I didn't bother.

The night was still and the sky clear. The stars shone quietly above our silent thoughts. Miami's humidity enveloped us while a few mosquitoes tormented us; but Tommie and I prevailed over the first discomfort with inactivity and prevailed over the second annoyance with an occasional slap.

A bit of spray dampened my left arm as a result of Tommie carelessly opening a can of beer. I guzzled what remained of my beer and reached for another.

Facing the rear of the house, we sat in the backyard on a pair of lawn chairs, sharing a six-pack. The house was dark except for Fran's bedroom. Occasionally, we could see her neurotic silhouette through the window shade. She was pacing the floor, erratically stopping, turning, halting, smoking, changing her direction whenever the mood or emotion struck her. She had wanted to be alone and there, before our eyes, was the result of her wish. French and Janet had gone out to get something to eat.

"She's not doing well, Llew."

"I know."

Hesitation occupied the following silence.

"I'm not doing well, Llew." Tommie shifted in his seat and drew closer to me. He pointed his can of beer at the only lighted window. "I think I could find myself in her." He waited. "Do you have any trouble with that, Llew?"

I didn't know how to answer him but I managed to say, "No trouble at all."

I didn't bother to tell him that it wasn't possible to find himself in someone else. I didn't bother to say that he was that someone else; that she was already him and him, she. I didn't bother to interpret the hieroglyphics of my present thoughts.

"She's not perfect," he continued with a justification. "But

119

neither am I."

I didn't bother to tell him that his imperfection was perfect. That her imperfection was perfect. I didn't bother to tell him that everything was alright, as it was; I didn't bother.

"Are you sure?" he persisted.

"About nothing. I'm sure," I said. But I wasn't sure, of course. I was still accepting most of these thoughts on faith. Jansen's faith; my intellect. I could hear Jansen screaming at me even now. "I don't want you to believe in anything! I want you to see for yourself! Sit! Look into your own nature! Stop thinking!"

Tommie appeared terribly mystified by my terse remark. He held his perplexed expression until he realized that I was not going to qualify myself. The expression slowly bled from his countenance.

"And I am nothing," he said solemnly. He drained half his beer in three swallows. "I'm not smart. I'm not successful. I'm not liked." He turned to me in earnest. "What is it about me, Llew? Why do people shy away from me? I'm a good guy. A nice guy." He pointed his beer can at her lighted window again. "I could love her." He threw himself against the backrest of his lawn chair. "I'm nothing. I pump gas for a living and play at going to school at a junior college. I'm going nowhere. Amounting to nothing. Becoming lonely."

He looked at me. He waited for an answer.

"I don't know what to tell you, Tom."

I didn't bother to tell him that he needed to throw his life away if he wanted to live; be this very moment of suffering if he wanted to escape it. I didn't bother to tell him that there was nothing to seek. And in the final analysis, I didn't bother to try to tell him anything of value because I didn't know anything myself; my thoughts would be nothing more than the sound of my confusing words. So, I didn't bother; for both our sakes. I drank my beer. I didn't bother.

Chapter 37
Intermezzo

This was not a party; this was a detached expression of our love. There was no way to cope other than face insanity itself. So, we all sat in our hooch, smoking weed and looking at the empty objects which represented Stacey: a narrow cot, a single footlocker filled with his personal possessions, a photograph of his girlfriend thumbtacked to the green plywood wall.

Emptiness prevailed; emotion would have been suicide. Stacey had been killed in action. Nonexistence existed.

We smoked. We stared. We did not talk about Stacey. Because everything was Stacey. Discipline prevailed.

> feeling strangely hollow
>
> Today
> wanting to call my father
> and listen to that soft sound of
>
> Yesterday
> wondering what has happened
> to the feeling for my life; in the
>
> Present
> I see the hopelessness
> that makes a failure of all, who are
>
> Mortal

*   *   *   *

Structure and discipline were the guiding forces of our behavior. We were dedicated students and we loved the world of academics. We were among the few who went to school for what I considered the right reason: for its own sake. Not to prepare ourselves for a job, not to learn a trade, not even to improve our skills in coping with the real world. We were complete students, without a past or a future. Attending the university was everything. Learning was everything. Academic performance was everything. In fact, our structure and discipline was monastic in perspective.

Everything took a back seat to our studies, everything: clothes, food, surroundings, ownership of things, everything—except for Friday night: our big night, our night to howl.

Me and her; I have to see it that way because that's the way it was—a self-centered world of me and her. God, were we wonderfully selfish. All week long we did exactly what we had chosen to do with our lives and, on our only evening of rest, we chose not to share ourselves with anybody else.

Howling meant going to the store together and buying an eighty-nine-cent bottle of Tickle Pink Wine and a large bag of potato chips. It was what we could afford and a single bottle of wine was all we needed to get the desired effect. At first, I was almost self-conscious about buying wine called Tickle Pink. The name assaulted my manly manhood and I would compensate by using a deeper voice and affecting a very masculine posture when purchasing the bottle at the store.

Catherine screeched with laughter when I did this and she made me laugh at myself. From then on, Tickle Pink became the code word which signified the beginning of our Friday night howl. In fact, I began strutting my manly manhood strut and saying "Tickle Pink" in my manly manhood voice as early as Friday morning in anticipation of that night. I got my best kisses from Catherine that way—God, we loved each other so.

Armed with Tickle Pink and potato chips, we drove home and turned on the television. It was the only time we ever watched television and we considered this activity wonderfully extravagant. Tickle Pink, potato chips, and a black and white television tuned to the only television station it was capable of transmitting was our form of extravagance. Oh, but did I forget to tell you about our joy, our youth, our comfort in simple things, our blind perceptions toward a beautiful world? What is extravagance without these? And did I forget to tell you about the passion of our love-making which followed?—not that love-making was restricted to a Friday night or even required; our love-making was direct and honest and exploring and sharing and wonderfully physical. Extravagance. I did not forget.

Hoping I would guess
    that she wanted us to make love
That's romance,
Wanting to go out
    if that would please me more instead
That's romance,
Afterwards coffee
    quite leisurely while still in bed
That's romance,
Walking and talking
    extending the day together
That's romance,
Wasting the evening
    over wine and potato chips
That's romance,
A hug and a kiss
    sincerely and expressly felt
That's romance:
All gentle moments;
    no more and no less for their own
Lovely sake.

Chapter 38
"I hate you."

I should have known better. Tommie and I should have known better. Frances couldn't have gone to sleep in her state of mind. She left us sitting in our relative darkness after she turned off the bedroom light. We sat drinking our beer, staring at her darkened window in a brain-damaged state. Our companionship had been reduced to the comfort of complete silence. Only many years of unquestioning friendship, the brotherhood of our growing up together, could allow this kind of silence to prevail over, beyond, and in between our personal shortcomings.

A long time passed before I began to become restless. Uneasiness invaded my condition when I started feeling a sense of vacancy from the house. Of course, all this was intangible and I was drunk and Tommie...was Tommie. But I couldn't help thinking that an occupied house felt different. I shot up to my feet.

"Something's wrong, Tom."

"French and Janet will be back anytime now."

"It's not that, man."

Tommie sensed my alarm.

"We've been staring at the darkness too long," I said.

"What?"

"Frances!" I exclaimed.

Tommie sprang up to his feet. He understood. His face was instantly clear and sober. He leaped ahead of me and reached the back porch first. Once inside, we flicked on every light switch we passed on our way to the bedroom. The last flood of light finally confirmed both our fears: Frances was trying to commit suicide again. She was lying on the bed with an empty bottle of Thorazine on one side of her and an empty can of beer on the other. She was still conscious; there was hope!

I grabbed her by the front of her tee shirt and pulled her up into a sitting position.

"You idiot!" Tommie squawked with concern the way a parent sometimes reacts during a crisis. Love can express itself in many ways.

"Take hold of her arm, Tom." He was on the verge of panic. "Tom!" The sound of his name had the desired effect.

"Sorry, Llew."

We sandwiched Frances between us and made her stand up as we supported her by her upper arms.

"Leave me alone," Frances babbled. Her speech was slurred and almost incoherent.

"Let's walk her to the bathroom," I said, ignoring her resistance.

"What are we going to do?" Tommie asked.

"No hospital," I said. "I think we can make it without the hospital, this time."

"I don't know, Llew."

"The police will arrest her this time," I said. Panic reappeared in Tommie's eyes. "Hurry. I don't think it's been long."

I brought Frances to her knees as soon as we reached the bathroom and bent her over the bathtub.

"Are you sure, Llew?"

"We'll know in a minute."

I pinched her nose and stuck the end of a toothbrush I found toward the back of her throat. She gagged. She clawed at my hands.

"Grab her arms, Tom!"

Tommie was responsive. I was successful. Frances was saved. She vomited. Completely. Painfully. Whole capsules of thorazine spewed from her mouth. They flowed from her in a sea of yellow foaming liquid which erupted from the depths of her bowels. I could feel the abdominal convulsions because my body was pressed against hers from behind. We must have looked a sight: Frances bent over with her stomach pressed against the edge of the tub, myself bent over on top of her pinching her nose and probing the back of her throat with the toothbrush, and Tommie bent over behind me in order to reach both sides of Frances to hold onto her arms.

She gagged, spat, coughed, gasped, gulped, puked, convulsed and finally—cried. But she vomited. Completely. Painfully. In the end, all she had left in her came out with the soft flow of sobbing amid intermittent clearings from the back of her throat and sniffles against the cloudy white substance which dripped from her delicate nostrils. She looked paler than ever, paler than death. Her close-cropped blonde hair was matted against her skull with perspiration.

Her body finally relaxed, completely spent, weakened by the trauma. When Tommie released her hands, she raised them to get hold of the bathtub's ledge for support.

"I hate you," she managed to say.

"I know," I said as I supported her head by pressing the palm of one of my hands against her forehead. Her upper body was still perpendicular to the tub with her head bowed toward her frothy vomit. She was now suffering with the dry heaves. Occasionally, she gasped painfully.

French and Janet's voices intruded upon this spectacle.

"Oh my god!"

"What happened?"

"Where have you two been?" Tommie asked without looking behind.

"Out," French said dumbly.

I reached for a towel and wiped Fran's face. When I turned around their expressions startled me. The horror of this scene was fully mirrored upon their faces. Suddenly, the light was too bright in this tile and porcelain world. Suddenly, the odor and spatter of her bodily excretions were everywhere. Suddenly, the realization of Fran's genuine attempt at suicide was evident.

"What are we going to do with her?" French inquired.

"Take care of her," Tommie blurted.

"Let's take her into the bedroom," I said.

"We're going to have to keep an eye on her all night," Tommie declared.

"Any of you mind taking their turn on watch?" I asked. The short silence that followed meant that everyone agreed to help. "Then I'll take the first watch," I volunteered.

"No, I'll take the first watch," Tommie said.

"Then I'll make some coffee," I said.

Frances heaved impotently one last time but nothing came out of her. Since my hand was still cradling her forehead, I felt the shudder of her spasm.

"The poor slob," Janet stated flatly without judgment, without any color to the tone of her voice. "I'll make the coffee. Just get her into the bedroom."

French scratched his head to physically emphasize his predicament.

"I guess I'm stuck with cleaning up this mess."

"I'll take care of it, French," I said earnestly.

"Naw, that's okay," he countered. "I'll do it. Besides, we all voted."

"For what?" Tommie inserted.

"For her," French continued. "She's one of us, remember?"

"Yeah," Tommie agreed.

Janet squeezed French's arm with approval, then left the bathroom to make us coffee. French was visibly pleased by Janet's behavior. Almost too pleased.

Chapter 39
I Thought

I made the decision not to take Frances to the hospital. The responsibility of that decision kept me up all night taking her pulse, watching her respiration and studying the pallor of her skin. Tommie never left the room either. After checking in once or twice, French went to bed while Janet fell asleep on the living room sofa. Frances was alright, physically. Psychologically? That was another story. Earlier, French had distilled the entire problem into one phrase. "What are we going to do with her?" I didn't know. How does one point to the value of life? I thought. How could I show her the moon without her looking at my finger pointing at the moon, instead? I wasn't a teacher. I didn't know what I was doing. All I knew was I had to keep my practice strong.

I looked out the window. Dawn was approaching. Tommie had finally dozed off. I picked up the spare pillow from the bed, folded it twice, held it down to the floor, and sat upon it.

Maybe. . .maybe I won't have to say anything to her.

I crossed my left leg under my right thigh and crossed my right leg over my left thigh into a half lotus position. My zazen progress to this point had been painful, everyday. But I had finally succeeded in achieving a half lotus; pain is always here.

If my practice is strong, I thought, she will see it.

"You don't have to talk about the dharma; you are the dharma." That's what Jansen once told me.

I centered myself. My hands came together into the mudra position and my thoughts whirled into a single incongruous thought.

the mist: raining up
as much as it is raining
down

I let go of that thought. I centered myself. I concentrated on my breath. . .I thought. . .I concentrated on my body. . .I thought. . .I concentrated on nothing. . .I thought. . .I. . .

Chapter 40
Sweetwater

Tommie stayed home from work to watch over Frances. I had planned to but Tommie insisted. I gladly relented. I really couldn't afford to lose my job. And not showing up one morning would have been sufficient grounds for sudden unemployment. Ted had made that clear on our first meeting.

The sun burned. And the oppressiveness of Florida's humidity was particularly vengeful this morning. The sun glared. And the brightness of its yellow spectrum was reflected on the vast field that we were mowing. It made my eyes squint. And in a short time, this squinting became more bitter because of the endless flow of my sweat stinging my eyes. No amount of wiping my forehead or my sponge-like eyebrows made any difference. My hatband was soaked and the shade from its brim was nonexistent. At least, that's how it felt.

We took our first break at ten o'clock that morning; it coincided with the completion of our first job for the day. There were no trees and it was too hot to sit in the cab; there was no escape from the sun. I pulled the brim of my bamboo hat lower across my forehead to deepen the shade for my eyes. Ted pointed to the pickup truck's canvas cover and together we pulled a portion of it across the opened tailgate to provide a measure of insulation against the heat of the vehicle's body. I was the first to sit down, more weary than thirsty. Ted reached into the ice chest, pulled out two soft drinks, and gave me one before he hoisted himself onto the tailgate beside me. We drank most of our sodas in silence with our legs dangling freely in the air.

When Ted finished his drink, he crushed the can and pitched it behind him into the back of the open pickup. He quietly chewed his tobacco for a moment, braced himself, then spit a wad of brown fluid a few feet away. He turned to me with a penetrating stare. I was exhausted and my eyes must have shown it.

"You're not going to quit on me, are you?" he asked.

"Not yet," I answered. "But I may be getting close."

"Sure going to miss you."

"Yeah."

"Do me a favor."

"Sure."

"Don't tell me when. Just...don't show up. Okay?"

"Okay," I said.

The long silence between us was comfortable. I could sense a change in him. I could tell his mind was reeling, almost conniving.

"I know a couple of women," he stated suggestively.

I hesitated before I answered. "And?" I finally coaxed.

"Would you like to meet them?"

"Why not?" I emphasized with the broad gesture of my hands.

"Come on," he said as he hopped off the tailgate. "Let's pack it in for the day. You're coming with me."

I didn't ask any questions. Anything was going to be better than work today. In a short time, we had the trailer and truck loaded and were cruising west on the Tamiami Trail alongside the Tamiami Canal. We took one quick turn up 107th Avenue and a left onto West Flagler Street.

"We're in Sweetwater if you're wondering," Ted announced.

"I've never had any reason to come up here," I said.

After a short while and a few more turns, we pulled into a driveway which led toward a magnificent house. It was a miniature estate, replete with a high surrounding fence and a dense landscaping of tropical trees and shrubbery. The architecture of the single-story house was distinctively Spanish. The house had white stucco walls, a terra cotta roof, and a horseshoe-shaped floor plan that created an open courtyard in the middle. A three-foot wall enclosed the courtyard and a six-foot stone arch with a wrought iron gate at the wall's midpoint served as the initial front entranceway. I looked at Ted with surprise. He smiled.

"Call me eccentric," he said.

What an understatement, I thought.

Ted stopped the vehicle in front of the courtyard. He spat the lump of tobacco, that always bulged from his cheek, out of his mouth as soon as he stepped off the truck.

"This way," he said.

I followed him through the courtyard and through the double-door main entrance into the interior of the house. I won't waste time in describing the inside of the home. Suffice it to say that it was as tropical inside as it was outside and as impeccably landscaped in Spanish decorum.

"You can shower in that bathroom over there," he said.

The croaking of his bullfrog voice was incongruous in these surroundings. He ambled toward the opposite end of the house looking like an untidy spider in this elegant environment and disappeared down a hallway.

I was floating. I was in paradise: cool, quiet, immaculately clean.

The spotless bathroom was fully equipped with toiletries, towels, and even a bathrobe. I took complete advantage of these provisions while luxuriously squandering my time. I came out of the guest bathroom and into the large Florida room clad in the long white terry cloth bathrobe I took from the back of the door. Ted was standing by a bar, also in a bathrobe, with two drinks poured. He had just hung up the telephone.

"I've got a couple of friends coming over to see us," he said.

I acknowledged this information with a smile. I felt a rush of anticipation.

"You like Bloody Marys?" he asked.

"They're okay in the morning," I said.

"Take one," he said.

I was surprised at the expanse of the room, once I began to walk across it. Skylights dotted the ceiling and flooded the room with natural sunlight. I sat down at the bar and took a sip of my drink.

"It's good," I said.

Ted looked different. His short and stocky, powerfully built frame seemed more genteel in these surroundings; his face seemed less malformed now that it was clean and shaven. His massive neck and the leathery brown skin of his upper chest were fully exposed by the opening of his robe while two very heavy legs protruded from the bottom of the garment. He was still using tobacco but in the form of a little black cigar. The smoke that curled from it smelled sweet. He looked completely comfortable.

Most people would have asked me what I thought of all this. Ted didn't. By the time we were halfway through our second

Bloody Mary, the doorbell rang. I remained seated while Ted answered the door.

The peal of laughter from two women was the first thing to assault me. Then came the garishness of primary colors from their long skirts and their halter tops. They were dark-complected brunettes in heavy make-up. And after a closer inspection, I realized that they were two over-the-hill prostitutes. One of them was Filipino and the other was Spanish. They shared two broad smiles between them. Their smiles were natural and not part of any kind of performance. By the sound of their heavily accented voices, they were genuine friends of Ted; or he was a very good and regular client of theirs. The Filipino was the smaller of the two and she took notice of me first. She let out an explosive cry of delight as she came over to me.

"Hello, honey. What's your name?"

Here we go, I thought. I smiled.

"Llew."

I finished my Bloody Mary while she snuggled up against me at the bar. The other woman linked herself around one of Ted's arms and allowed him to escort her to the bar.

"Llew," he said. "That fine lady you have beside you is Elena and this is Margaritta.

"Hello," I said, rather blankly. I held a painted smile on my face, not knowing what else to do.

Ted stepped around the bar to make the ladies a drink. He croaked happily at me for my approval and at the girls for a display of their charms. He was successful on both counts: the ladies laughed and I croaked back at him with my endorsement. He was amused at my imitation of him.

We occupied ourselves with a happy and relaxed preamble of small talk and sexual innuendo. I could see that this was part of their well-established ritual that would eventually lead to the more physical act of foreplay. Ted was harmlessly lecherous. The girls loved him. I got the distinct impression that, on more than one occasion, the three of them had shared the same bed. It was like one happy family and I was included.

I had several Bloody Marys in me, a clean terry cloth robe wrapped around me, and an enthusiastic lady to entertain me. I don't think there was anything missing.

"How do you like these girls?" Ted boasted as he sat down in an easy chair and had Margaritta sit on his lap.

"I love them," I said.

Ted crudely, but gently, reached into Margaritta's halter top and pulled out one of her large breasts. It didn't seem to bother her in the least.

"Ain't that just beautiful?" he croaked as Margaritta giggled proudly.

I didn't know what to say. But my astonished expression seemed to amuse him. And that's all the answer he wanted or needed to see.

I abruptly found myself occupied with my Filipino lady. I had to look down to confirm the sensation. Elena had placed one of her hands between my thighs and was stimulating me to an erection. I looked at her. I must have grinned. I was speechless. She wasn't. She released a foreign hiss from between her teeth that was oddly seductive and said something provocative to me in a language I did not understand. In the midst of our interplay, I realized that the single organism comprising our group had divided itself in mitosis fashion to form two complete cellular organisms that were functioning quite independently of each other.

I didn't have to do anything. Elena was an aggressive expert; her sexual advances demanded all my attention.

I vaguely remembered hearing Ted say something about the availability of bedrooms and that Elena knew the way to all of them. I think I nodded. I think Ted laughed. I think I was glad Ted brought me to Sweetwater.

Chapter 41
"She rejected me."

Ted dropped me off at the donut shop late in the afternoon. The routine conclusion of our day together was a fitting end. I suspected that Ted really didn't want to know where I lived and consequently didn't really want to know who I was. He gave me a full day's pay, told me not to spend it all in one place, and drove off expecting to see me ready for work in the morning. I pocketed the money and decided to go into the donut shop for a cup of coffee. I found Tommie sitting at the counter waiting for me. I didn't bother to ask him what he was doing here.

"What'll you have?" he asked.

"Coffee," I answered.

He translated that into sign language to the waitress standing at the other end of the counter.

"I didn't see your car in the parking lot," I said.

"I walked over here," he said. I waited for the rest of his answer. "Janet's feeling a little guilty about Willie and borrowed my car to look for him. She left before French came home from work. She didn't want him to come with her."

"I can understand that."

"Yeah, me too. Anyway, French is looking after Frances right now. I had to get out of there. Too much death talk between her and Willie."

"Willie?"

"Janet. Same thing. She's worried about what he might do to himself. She's just as miserable as Willie."

"I think she's trying to do something about that."

"I think French is trying to do something about that," Tommie said. I was still uncommitted.

"Maybe," I said.

The waitress placed a cup of coffee in front of me. I thanked her with a nod.

"I'm going to California, Llew."

I sensed we were approaching the reason for his being here.

"Why California?"

"I don't know, I. . .I spent the day with her, Llew. She rejected me."

"Give her some time. What do you expect?"

"I don't know. I don't want to know."

He shoved his coffee away as if he were shoving himself away.

"She's afraid of life," I said. "And you give up too easily."

"She wants you."

"She doesn't know what she wants."

"She's still your girl."

"And I don't know what I want."

Tommie was skeptical.

"You need to talk to her about that," he said.

"I know. As soon as I know how. But, for now, you've got to get to know her."

"But what is she?"

"A person," I said, "who's reaching out. I'm the one who happened to be out there on the beach. I'm the one who found her. It could have been anybody. I know that now."

"You mean, you don't love her?"

"Of course I do. But not in the same way. Not in your way."

Tommie shifted in his seat uneasily. "Don't feel bad," I continued.

Tommie was staring at the counter top.

"Stay in Miami, Tom. Frances needs somebody," I finally said, implying that he was the one she really needed.

Tommie raised his head with resolve.

"I'm going to have to think, Llew."

"Think."

"I'm leaving for a few days. Tell French not to worry."

"Where are you going?"

"Out."

"Okay," I said with understanding. "But don't run away to California or anything like that. Promise?"

"I promise."

How did I get myself into this mess, I thought. All these relationships. People. What a mess. Was this the meaning of life, too?

Chapter 42
"You made me hurt you."

Tommie and I walked home. We noticed that his car was parked in the driveway.

"Janet didn't let herself go very far," he said flatly.

"And neither have you," I said. "Don't forget that."

My remark seemed to startle him out of his trance.

"Maybe you're right," he said somewhat introspectively. He got into his car. The keys were still in the ignition. "I'll pick up some of my things. . .when nobody's around."

"Don't stay away too long."

"I won't. I promise. A week, maybe."

He started the car and drove away leaving me feeling a little empty. There was nothing left for me to do but go into the house.

I heard them speaking as soon as I walked through the front door. The voices that were French and Janet came from the kitchen. I remained silent in the living room, unable to resist. I quietly shut the door behind me and listened. The vocal intensity between them was strained. It was obvious they had not heard Tommie drive away or me enter the house.

The sound of their words went like this.

"Why do you keep trying to help that jerk?" French asked imploringly.

"Because he's still my husband," she said defensively.

"You could have gone to jail for helping him go AWOL when you did."

"I didn't know he was in the trunk of my car."

"Cute," French remarked peevishly. "You think the gate guards would have believed you if they had searched your vehicle?" She didn't answer. I could almost envision her defiant eyes; loyal eyes. "Those Camp Lejune Marines don't play, Janet." More silence.

I could smell resentment. I knew Janet well enough to know that it was alright for her to complain about Willie but not alright for anyone else to do the same. Even if it was in her best interest; even if it was French.

"I don't want to talk about this anymore, French."

"Willie is no good for you, Janet."

"And I don't want you to say anything more about him."

"I'm sorry."

There was a long silence.

"No, French, not now."

"You know how I feel about you."

Janet's voice trembled.

"French. . .no."

I heard the sound of a slap. Another silence followed. Now the voices between them sounded more distant. French spoke first.

"He slaps you and now you slap me."

"He slapped me once."

"I love you. I always have."

"Please, French. You and me, well. . .I'm not sure it's possible."

French flew off indignantly.

"At least I'd be faithful!"

Janet refused to answer him. French regained control of himself and attacked her very softly.

"He doesn't even love you."

Janet verified the truth of French's cruel statement with several audible sniffles. I heard French physically approach her.

"I'm sorry," he said.

"Go away. No. Wait." French quietly waited. "It's no secret that I'm fed up with Willie. And I guess it's no secret to you that I don't love him anymore."

"But he's never loved—"

"Don't say it. . .again. I don't want to hear it."

French was determined to say what he was thinking even if it was going to ruin whatever chances he hoped to have in securing a permanent relationship with Janet.

"I hate Willie for what he's done to you."

"French. Don't hate. It doesn't become you."

I could tell that French was becoming exasperated.

"Don't look at me like that," she said. "He is unfaithful. He doesn't love me. He is a loser." Her tone was almost capricious.

"But I don't have the heart. . .to hate him. I. . .we. . .can be friends, you and I. . ." She reacted peevishly. "No. French!"

"I was just going to hug you."

"I don't love you." I could almost feel French's pain during the lull that followed. "Not in the way you want me to. You see? You made me hurt you."

"I don't care," French responded heroically. "I can wait. You can change."

Janet sighed.

"We'll see."

I backed up to the front door knowing that this break in their conversation was a good place to interrupt them. I slammed the door pretending to come into the house and walked across the living room with some fanfare. When I walked into the kitchen, I found the two of them standing in front of the refrigerator facing each other at arm's distance. Janet's cheeks were tear- stained with mascara and French's face was painted with regret.

"How is Frances?" I asked, ignoring the uneasiness between them and the embarrassment of my presence.

"She's fine," Janet answered. "She's in the bedroom listening to the radio."

"We were just getting ready to go out to eat," French said. "Want to come?"

"No thank you," I said politely.

We all avoided each other's eyes. And in so doing, we all acknowledged the restiveness between us. French and Janet stood planted on the ground as if they were afraid to move; as if by moving they would have to expose themselves to me. I rescued them by stirring first.

"Think I'll check in on Frances."

As soon as I left the kitchen and disappeared down the hallway, I heard them scurry across the living room and out the front door.

Complicated, I thought. More people. What a mess. I suppose neatness is a concept, too.

Chapter 43
"Crazy. I must be crazy."

The radio was playing softly and Frances was lying on the bed. She must have fallen back to sleep because she did not stir when I entered the room.

I tip-toed to the closet and brought out a clean pair of jeans which I hooked onto the doorknob. Even though I had bathed at Ted's house, the clothes I wore for work this morning were dirty.

I peeled off all my clothes and dropped them onto the floor. As I stood there naked, I smelled Elena's strong sexual scent. I had not taken another shower after our afternoon of love-making. The affair had ended as abruptly as it had begun, with Ted ushering us all out of his house like a farmer shooing a bunch of chicks off a front porch. Of course, I didn't care. But I had to chuckle. Ted was acting as if he were answerable to someone else. A wife, perhaps? I chuckled.

The flat of a hand gently touching my back startled me. I turned around.

"I wasn't asleep," she said.

"You were pretending?"

"That's right."

Frances took a step closer, leaned toward me, and gave me a kiss. I gently broke away from her. She spoke softly, almost too sensuously.

"I want you, Llew. I want you inside me."

I didn't answer her. I don't know why.

"You don't find me sexually attractive," she said.

"It's not that at all."

She sat down at the edge of the bed. I felt compelled to follow her. I pulled on my jeans and sat beside her. I did not put my arms around her. I did not touch her.

"How do you feel?" I asked.

"Like shit," she answered. "It's because of Drew, isn't it?"

"Don't be silly. It's because of me."

I began to feel the extent of my rejection upon her. I reached over the bed and turned off the radio.

"I'm afraid, Frances. Afraid to make a commitment with you."

"Hey, there are no strings attached to our having sex."

"That's a lie."

Her eyes were full, crystal blue, and liquid in depth.

"I suppose you're right," she said. "Okay, no sex. So. . .besides making me crazy, what's next?"

"You want to try something different?"

"We've been doing a pretty good job with 'different' if you ask me."

"It's called zazen," I said.

"Za what?"

"Zazen."

"What is that?"

"It's nothing. It's doing nothing."

Confusion reigned over her countenance. I laughed. I knew I was going to confuse her more.

"You don't achieve anything with zazen. You don't become holy, or spiritual, or happier, or healthier, or smarter, or powerful, or better than anybody else."

By now, both her hands were in a fist and braced against her hips with her arms akimbo.

"Alright," she said in a vocal challenge that dared me to go on.

"Zazen is sitting," I said. "It is a simplified space. It is coming back into the stillness of your center. . .you. Because zazen is about you. It is meditation about ourselves."

"Oh, it's meditation." She sounded disappointed. "Is that all."

"Have you ever done it?" I challenged.

"Well. No."

"Have you ever stopped thinking for a few minutes?"

"What's so important about that?"

"That. . .is part of the reason you desire to kill yourself."

"What would you know about my reasons?" She said defensively.

"I'm sorry. I really don't know your reasons."

"And what's so hard about za. . .meditation."

"Nothing," I said. "You want to do it with me?"

She smiled.

"I tried to a few minutes ago," she said.

I grinned.

"You know what I meant. Zazen. You want to do it?"

"Okay," she said with an opaque smirk. "But. . .with zazen, what is supposed to happen?" She insisted. "What do you become?"

I risked answering her with a word.

"Clearer."

I waited for the word to penetrate her.

"Are you ready to try it?" I continued.

"Sure. What have I got to lose?"

"There is a secret to life," I said as I got a blanket out of the closet and folded it lengthwise for thickness. "But it's not a secret. It's something that has been in front of you all your life." I gathered up our bed pillows and placed them over the folded length of blanket. "They sometimes call it enlightenment. But trusting in things being as they are is all enlightenment is."

"That's a hell of a secret," Frances retorted skeptically.

"I know," I said. "So why doesn't everybody see it?"

This question intrigued her. And before she could recover, I had her standing in front of one of the pillows I had placed at each end of the blanket.

"There," I said. "Are you ready?"

"What do you want me to do?"

"First of all, stop talking; inside and out."

She nodded.

I folded a pillow in half and held it in place over the thickness of the folded blanket.

"Sit on this."

She sat.

"Good."

I went over to my pillow, folded it in the same way, and sat on it. We were facing each other.

"Now do as I do."

I put my left leg under my right thigh. She did it. I put my right foot over my left thigh. She did it. Easily. I suspected she was so limber that she could probably do a full lotus without any effort. I had to remind myself that this in itself was no achievement. The pain in the legs, while sitting in zazen, was greater for some people than for others. The pain was always there for me, for instance, while there was no apparent pain displayed in Fran's face. Then again, what was pain? Never mind that. Instead, I'll tell you what it's not: it's not suffering. And suffering was what registered on Fran's face in the form of suicide.

Was suicide easier than doing this? I thought.

"Good," I said. "Now straighten your back. Good. Lift your head. Good. Tuck in your chin. Good. Partially close your eyes if you can. Good. Place your tongue against the upper part of your palate and behind your front teeth. Got it? Good. Now place the back of your left hand into your right palm with your thumbs barely touching, like this. Good. Now die."

"What?"

"Never mind," I said.

I had to do that, I thought. I remembered Jansen planting that seed into me in the same way. "Calm yourself into death," Jansen later amplified to me. I ended my silent thoughts by speaking Jansen's words aloud to Frances.

"Everybody is caught up in the whirlwind of life. Everybody. But gradually, through zazen, the whirlwind calms; it is a step toward death. Anytime we are caught in this whirlwind, we have not died. Needing is a whirlwind. Seeing in a particular way is a whirlwind. Wanting approval is a whirlwind. Having died means no whirlwind. But who is without it? All that most of us can do is to sit down in zazen and be as we are at this point in time. Be perfect: in zazen and out of zazen for as long as we can. Understand?"

"No."

"Good," I said.

Wasn't that what Jansen told me? I thought. I'm such a poor teacher. I'm not a teacher at all. Forgive me, I said to myself, not knowing of whom or what I was asking forgiveness. But I had to act, I thought. I had to do something for Fran's sake.

"Suicide is an attachment, Frances. Sitting like this is the only way to die. All you can be is what you are right now."

"Crazy. I must be crazy."

"Then be crazy. Sit with that thought until it is no longer there. Until you are no longer there."

Silence finally prevailed as we continued to sit.

Chapter 44
Intermezzo

Our hooch was constructed with sheets of plywood, which served as our floors and walls, nailed onto a skeleton of two by four frames and topped with a tin roof. A continuous window ran the length of both sides of the structure with a shelf running the interior length of its sill. This shelf provided a place for us to lay out a few personal articles. There was no glass, only a metal screen nailed over the opening to keep the bugs out and to provide cross ventilation. A screened-in door at each end of the hooch completed the major structural aspect to our abode.

Concerning habitability, our hooch was kept clean and in reasonable order. Our webbed gear and weapons hung from nails protruding from the rafters. And each man had a cot and a locker which defined his space. Approximately sixteen men lived in a hooch; two eight-man teams.

There was no thought of privacy; none existed, none was needed. We lived together because we died together. This was truly a collective consciousness comprised of individuals as diverse as the human race. And nothing made this consciousness more felt than the approach of night, when loneliness prevailed and held all of us captive.

We either had recently returned from a patrol or were preparing to go back out. Patrols. It is also what we talked about and thought about and were afraid to dream about. So, sleeplessness prevailed until enough booze and smoke brought us far enough away from ourselves.

Funny. In the bush, I can clearly remember coming to terms with myself before falling asleep; I always accepted never waking up as I drifted toward slumber. But when I was back in my hooch, I don't ever remember falling asleep.

I understand! I understand! loving. . .
I understand the moisture of the earth
I understand the sweet caress of the living
by the sorrows of animals and man.

I see the burden of our touching
I see the burden of being touched
I see the burden of having been touched
by someone or something, that someday
will cease to exist.

So I cry for the future that is mine
And I cry for that future beyond my life
I cry for the future that lies before us all
I cry and I cry for this life of pain
this life of suffering
this life of the ordinary with its quiet touch
of death.

*   *   *   *

921 South Duval Street was the address of our second home. It was a beautiful little house that we rented for ninety-five dollars a month. The house was a single-story wooden frame structure that was painted white. The house had no air conditioning but it was unnecessary. Large pecan trees surrounded the house and kept our place relatively cool in the summer. For winter, we had a floor furnace which kept us warm. And for autumn and spring, we had a front and back porch to welcome those seasons. We had a kitchen with lots of windows, a bathroom that worked, and a furnished dining room, living room, and two bedrooms. We even had sheer white curtains which blew lazily with the seasonal breezes. We had, we had, we had.

I believe 921 was the most magical place that Catherine and I ever lived in. I don't think we ever locked our front door. And I don't think I ever forgot when I fell asleep.

Winter:
a private season

cloaked with longer evenings of darkness
feeling
    at one with the universe.
Spring:
a naked season
abundant with the coming of life
feeling
    alive with the universe.
Summer:
a constant season
relentless with the sun and the rain
feeling
    mortal with the universe.
Autumn:
a mystic season
bathed with the wind of eternal change
feeling
    alone with the universe.

Chapter 45
All Words

Willie appeared. He stood in the doorway, motionless, framed by the rectangular opening. The living room was dark, darker than the dusk that served as Willie's background, making him a shadow. Neither of us switched on a light. I waited. And while we lingered within the intensity of our silence, I could hear Frances taking a shower after our long session of zazen. When Willie finally spoke, his tone was so strained I barely recognized his voice.

"Where's Janet?"

"With French," I said.

I could not see the expression on his face. His countenance was a blend of grays and purples; a muddy shadow reflecting the mind that was the source of this image: Willie.

"Frances is trying to kill herself," Willie stated flatly as if this were news to me. It made me feel uneasy. It made me realize the seriousness of Willie's condition, whatever that was.

"So is Willie," I said.

My accusation had no effect on him.

"But I will succeed on my first real attempt," he said firmly.

He stepped through the door and solidified into flesh and blood.

"Is there anything I can do?" I asked. "Is there a doctor that I can take you to? Anything."

"Nothing. You've said so yourself. There's nothing."

When did I say this to him? I wondered.

"That nothing is not oblivion," I said. "You misunderstood me."

Has he been lurking by our windows at night listening to our conversation? I wondered.

"Willie, you're beginning to worry me." I was hesitant. But I had to ask. "Why? Why suicide?"

"I'm not happy."

"Happiness is a concept. It's not the truth."

"I want happiness," he said angrily.

"You can't dictate happiness because it doesn't exist."

"What's wrong with the concept of happiness?"

"In itself? Nothing. Concepts like happiness are necessary if we are to function. But that's not the problem. The problem arises when we insist that it is a truth. Nothing has to be; nothing is. And that's alright. Otherwise, we run around wanting everything; changing everything."

"I want it!" he screamed as if he were in tremendous pain.

"I know," I said rather softly in an effort to neutralize some of the intensity between us. "You're trying to want the greatest concept of all, yourself. You're trying to make life fit your concept of yourself. We all do it. And we all suffer for it."

Willie kneaded his temples in an attempt to soothe away some of the pressure that seemed to be building up within his cranium.

"What do you get out of all this? Why should you care what happens to me?"

"I'm not sure I do, I'm sorry to say."

Willie was stunned. He roared with laughter.

"You're the most honest bastard I know, I'll grant you that."

I had him interested, I thought. I had to keep trying. A story about Jansen came to the rescue.

"I lived with this guy called Jansen while I was in Baltimore last winter."

"That's the time when you disappeared after Catherine's death," he qualified.

"Yeah. It was after her death. I went crazy. You know that. I'd been married all my life."

I stood there thinking about my wife. Funny how much power her memory still had over me.

"And?" he prodded.

"And, I learned a lot from this guy Jansen. He taught me that we were all connected in some way. I am you and you are me. We are one. At least, that's one of the things he taught me before he died. That's the reason why I should care about you."

"And you believe in this drool?"

"Well. . .it is something I'm not sure about, because I haven't seen this. . .one. I guess this is the part of me that is religious. Because it is the part of me I have accepted on faith. Because

Jansen told me. Because Jansen knew. Because he encouraged me
to have my doubts until I could see for myself."

"Then I can't call you crazy," Willie said.

"Why?"

"Because according to you, it's not the truth."

"It's also not a concept."

Willie looked confused.

"Concept is also a word," I qualified.

"We need words," Willie insisted.

"Sure we do. It's when we separate ourselves from them that
we get into trouble. That's when we suffer."

"I have to step back from things so that I can see—"

"What I want," I finished.

"So? I want. I want happiness. I want fulfillment. I want success.
I want love. I want my freedom!"

"I want, I want, I want," I said. "There's not a word for giving
in your vocabulary."

"I give!"

"You misunderstand me." The expression on his face demanded
that I explain myself. "Total commitment to your life is what I
mean by giving. When you're able to completely give yourself,
pour yourself into the present moment, there won't be any more
suffering. Even when you experience pain, completely. . .there is
joy."

"Words. All words. You said so yourself," he accused.

"You're right," I said, feeling inadequate; knowing that Jansen
would have never indulged me in this manner.

"Come on," he said.

"Where to?" I asked.

"Let's go out and get drunk."

"Sure," I said, not knowing how else to stay with him. But I had
to take a stab at getting him to do zazen. "But wait."

I walked over to the sofa and dragged some of the cushions onto
the floor.

"What are you doing?" Willie inquired.

"Have you ever heard of zazen?" I asked.

"Don't try any of that meditation crap on me. I saw what you
were doing with Frances."

That confirmed my suspicion. He was prowling around the

house looking in on our activity. My skin crawled.

"Willie, please, let me help you."

"Nothing doing. I'm a Marine. I don't need that bull shit."

Willie was a plethora of incongruities. I stepped over the cushions and approached him.

"What about Janet?"

"Fuck Janet. Better yet. Let French fuck her."

There was no love in Willie's eyes. I didn't know what to say to that.

"Then let's get drunk," I blurted.

"Honest?"

"Honest."

He started to lead the way out but I grabbed him by the arm.

"Why suicide?" I asked soberly.

His eyes penetrated mine.

"I can't get it out of my mind: life is not worth living. I don't care if the earth revolves around the sun. Life has no meaning. I don't care that the world has three dimensions. Life is a lie. I don't care that there is order in the universe. Life is absurd." Then he said simply, "When I decide to die. . .I will."

"I will what?" Frances gaily interjected as she walked into the living room and switched on the overhead light.

"Get drunk before the night is gone," Willie answered as he flinched at the flood of light.

"Can I come?" she asked.

"Of course you can," Willie answered.

"I want to have fun," she said to him.

"We all want to have fun," Willie shouted. "Right, Llewellen?"

"Right," I said.

It was the three of us now. . .together. . .riding in a Mustang. . .together. . .ignoring the consequences of our actions. . .together. . .caught in the whirlwind of wanting.

Chapter 46
Gentle Fragments

The darkness of Monday morning was illuminated by the single candle I had provided. I was proud of Frances. Her zazen posture was good. But she was not quite as limber as I thought she was the other day. I could see pain registered in her face. But I could also see determination. I wanted to tell her that she really didn't need to sit in the half lotus position but I didn't have the heart. She needed that pain. It was giving her focus. We sat through three half-hour sessions with two ten-minute exercise breaks which I substituted with walking zazen, called kenhin.

Afterwards, she wanted some verbal instructions. But I did not indulge her. She had enough mental clutter without me adding any more. So, I elected to take a safer approach since she did not come to zazen because she was searching. All I could hope for was clarity. . .my clarity. All I could hope to give her was my transparency. I sat in front of her, knowing she would glance at me from time to time, and tried to forget everything that was on my mind. When she looked up, all she saw was an empty mind. All she received was no opinions. Of course, I didn't know what I was doing. But I was trying to be careful. I knew that my treatment of her was safe if I simply pointed at her own inner reality; made her look at that and not me. Nothing extra; right, Jansen? Nothing distinguishable. Morning zazen was over.

"I'm going to have to leave you here alone," I said. "Are you going to be alright? Can I trust you not to do anything foolish?"

"I'll overdose on soap operas; I promise," she said.

Her voice sounded firm and convincing.

"Good," I said. "Let's give it a whole week. Then we'll find you another job. Okay?"

She nodded.

I kissed her on the cheek and gave her a hug. There was nothing more I could do for her. There was nothing I could do for anybody. Tommie was gone. Willie kept disappearing. French was preoccupied with Janet. And Janet was preoccupied with Willie. And me? I had to get to work on time.

* * * *

I ignored the sun, the noise of the lawn mower, and myself. I drove the mower across the large field in a straight line but not with a straight mind. I was filled with disturbing thoughts that became a series of questions. My lips actually moved and made all the sounds.

"What is suicide? Why do people refuse to talk about it? Why is there so little known about it? Why do we, as rational beings, have a death-instinct? Why are none of us immune to this? Why are all of us killing ourselves in some chosen manner? Why is the price of life so high and why have we placed ourselves in that position? Why do we accuse external forces as the culprit? Why don't we look at the internal forces? And finally, why does somebody choose to end his life? Can anybody truly believe in an afterlife?"

I hunched down into the seat of the riding lawn mower and leveled my eyes dead ahead.

"We are animals. Do animals fear death? We are animals. Does suicide draw the line between a rational human being and, let's say, the instincts of a dog? I have to find out. I have to talk to Willie. I have to do something."

* * * *

After Ted drove away, I noticed that Willie was sitting in his red Mustang. He was parked in front of the donut shop waiting for me to get off work. I could see that he was looking at me through his rearview mirror but he didn't get out of his car. I approached the vehicle on the passenger side and peered through the open window.

"Sure good to see you, Willie," I said as I took off my hat and wiped my brow.

I forgot about the effect of this day, the protracted exposure to its heat. I was no longer exhausted.

"Hop in," Willie said.

Willie handed me a cold beer from a Styrofoam ice chest he had in the back seat as soon as I slammed the door shut. We both opened our fresh beers together and took long cool drinks. Throughout this time, I was carefully studying Willie. He did not look good. His face had a sickly pallor to it. He seemed anxious. I threw my hat onto the back seat.

"How have you been, Will?"

"You mean, where have you been, Will?"

"Janet has been worried."

"Quit the small talk, Llew."

I took a sip from my beer and waited. A short silence developed between us. I sat calmly watching Willie bite his fingernails. Until now, this habit had escaped my attention. But the constancy of this minor self-mutilation went beyond mere frequency. He bit into his digits quite savagely, almost cannibalistically. I'm sure he was not aware of what he was doing or how often. Upon closer inspection, I could see that he had gnawed off almost all of his nails from his fingers. In some cases, he was actually tearing at the skin itself and exposing the subcutaneous pink. And on his left little finger I finally saw him penetrate into the depth of red; blood! Was he chewing his nails or eating himself? I wondered.

"Don't your fingers hurt?" I asked.

"Yeah," Willie said. "It makes me feel good." He became self-absorbed. I waited for him to continue speaking.

"Remember that time I shot myself in the stomach while cleaning my twenty-two?"

I understood Willie's implication immediately.

"It wasn't an accident," I said without surprise.

"No," Willie said.

"A death wish even then," I said thinking aloud.

"I'm going to die anyway, Llew. Life is killing me. I walk in syrup. I'll be the master of life and death if I kill myself."

"That's an illusion, man."

"No, it's omnipotence."

"That's a delusion. Death."

"Death is not real if there is an afterlife."

There was no arguing that point if Willie truly believed in what he just said. That death was part of life was certainly true, of course. But an afterlife? I wasn't sure—

"I want to kill myself," Willie added. "But I don't want to die."

"Who are you really trying to kill, Willie?"

I hit a nerve.

"Why. . .myself, naturally."

I shook my head. I blindly stabbed into his darkness.

"Something. . .or someone else." I pointed my finger at him. I took a chance. "You can't kill Janet, so you're going to kill yourself."

"You're crazy," he said.

I hit something. I was on the target, somewhere. I could tell that there was an element of truth in my accusation. He became visibly agitated. He clasped both hands together into a large fist in order to hide the fact that they were shaking. I decided to reverse his words and use them against him as a form of shock therapy. I was not aware of the danger.

"And you're wrong about what you said earlier. You want to die. But you don't want to kill yourself. You cannot escape the necessity to continue with life."

"Why should I live?" Willie challenged.

"Why should you die?" I countered.

"It has to be easier than this lie. . .this hopelessness. . .this purposelessness. . .this constant pain."

"But you lose the argument with suicide," I said.

"No," he said. "That's my final insult to existence. I win."

Willie started the car. I did not ask him where we were going.

He drove recklessly. On the highway, he drove too fast. But he released his foot from the accelerator when he saw me finally buckle my seat belt. A thin glistening stream from each eye ended with a teardrop that hung on each cheek. He swiped them away as quickly as they had appeared. I remained silent.

"You're a good friend, Llew."

"I haven't done anything," I said.

"Nobody else would have been willing to die with me."

"Nobody else was here."

"Anything you say."

Willie obeyed the speed limit all the way back to French's house. And after I got out of the car, he handed me a beer before he opened one for himself. We drank deeply. Then Willie tossed me my hat and drove away without waiting for the advice I could not give him.

*   *   *   *

Frances and I sat late into the night doing zazen. And just when I thought my mind was settled, a terrible thought pierced my consciousness and stirred the dust from within. The thought had come from the effects of Willie. He was part of a dream and in this dream he was laughing as he spoke.

"Everybody wants to kill himself," he said. "They just don't know it."

It was the only thing he said to me during our quiet trip back to French's house. I don't know why his statement took so long to affect me but now Willie's remark stunned me momentarily. His statement made me tumble backward in time, in dream, in memory: did Jansen kill himself?

The passing thought horrified me. I remembered Jansen's insistence that he was alright; that there was no need for a doctor. No hospitals. He had been emphatic about that. In the end, there was only time to comfort him with the holy place that I could describe to him; that Catholic church where I had seen him do zazen for the first time. Think. Think! Jansen could not have killed himself!

I mastered my thoughts by concentrating on my sagging posture. I straightened my back and held myself steady.

Frances had been watching. She was still looking outward instead of within. I didn't say anything because I was a poor example. Frances was a good student; I was a poor instructor.

*   *   *   *

Our zazen blended into sleep and into more zazen the following Tuesday morning. There were fewer words between Frances and me. And by skipping breakfast that morning, I encouraged her to continue with her comfortable silence.

I got to the donut shop's parking lot just as Ted drove up.

"You're early," I said.

"Want coffee?"

"How did you know?" I smiled.

Ted bought coffee and donuts. I offered to pay for them but he told me that my money was no good. It was fortunate that I was able to get a little breakfast after all because I don't think I could have made it through the day without it.

Once we started work, the day was so grueling that I don't think Ted and I exchanged more than three words. Fortunately, we had grown used to each other's habits, had begun to understand each other's body language, had become comfortable with the general silence between us. It was a silence brought upon us through monotony, strenuous work, and the heat. This was another kind of existence.

As usual, Ted dropped me off at the donut shop's parking lot on Bird Road. I usually sprang out of the truck as soon as he came to a stop and waited for him to hand me my pay through the window. But today I had no spring left. I knew Willie would be waiting for me somewhere around here. I knew I had no answers for him. I felt helpless.

I remained in my seat as I scanned the parking lot looking for a hint of Willie's figure.

"Here," Ted rasped. "Hard day today."

As soon as I accepted the money from him, I had to look at the small bundle. I was surprised. Ted paid me double my salary.

"This is too much money, Ted."

"Shut up and take it," Ted said. "Call it a raise."

"But—"

"Take it."

"Thanks, Ted."

"For what," Ted croaked, pretending to be irritated. "You're a good worker. Don't look at me that way. I'll see you in the morning."

He turned away and waited for me to get out of the truck.

"Ted. You're okay."

Ted grunted. He didn't know how to take a compliment. He drove away as soon as I got out of the truck.

I stood motionless, watching the vehicle disappear into the distance of Bird Road. Then I began to look for Willie. He was not sitting in his car nor was he in the donut shop. I walked around the side of the building and continued around toward the back, where

I found him standing at the rear of the shop underneath the only piece of shade made available by an aluminum awning over a door. His wry smile penetrated me.

"I knew you'd find me," he said.

"I had no choice," I said. Willie pulled out a half-pint of bourbon and offered me a drink. "No thanks." I believe he expected my refusal and was already sucking on the bottle. "I'm getting worried about you, Willie."

"Somebody has to," he said.

"Is there anything I can do?"

"No. Besides, nothing ever goes right for me anyway. I join the Marine Corps and look: I'm AWOL; hell, I'm probably classified a deserter, now. I go to school and look: I fail. I get married and look: I'm impotent."

There it was, I thought. The source of his misery. Impotence. The importance of sexuality.

"But that wouldn't matter with Janet," I said. "Isn't she. . ."

"Of course Janet's understanding! She's so understanding it makes me sick!" Willie shuddered. "She makes me feel like an invalid. . .retarded. . .half a man. I can't look in the mirror."

"There are treatments for that kind of disorder."

"Ha! Now it's a disorder!"

"To know thyself—"

"Is to hate thyself."

"Is to be awake."

Willie finished off the bottle and looked at it as if he just discovered it in his hand.

"Why do I drink so much?" Willie ignored his own question. He pitched the empty bottle into a small clump of bushes. "When Janet and I used to make love it was great. She loved it."

"And what about you?" I asked.

"I had some pleasure."

Willie did not sound very convincing.

"And. . ."

Willie was reluctant.

"And I always had to think of other women while we. . ."

"There's nothing wrong with that," I said after I realized he was not going to finish his statement.

Willie was not listening to me. He chuckled to himself instead.

"The last time she tried to make love with me, I played along. I wanted to do it. I really did. We kissed and got naked and. . .and. . .I pretended I was going to. I got between her legs holding myself. I couldn't help myself. She was looking at me so fucking patiently. I looked right back at her. And do you know what I did? I pissed on her." Willie laughed hysterically. He stopped. The abruptness of the following silence was unsettling. "She wasn't angry. She was surprised. I soiled her and she was surprised. Bitch! I hate her!" He broke down and began to cry. "I love her; I hate myself; I need a drink."

Willie tramped away unsteadily, intoxicated with bitterness. I couldn't call out after him. I simply walked home.

* * * *

Frances was sitting in the living room watching a talk show. I could smell food. I took off my hat and dropped it on one of the living room chairs.

"I made dinner for everybody today," she said. She got up from the sofa and turned off the television. "What's wrong? You look worried."

"I'm sorry it shows," I said.

"That's alright," she said. "But now you've got to talk to me."

Good, I thought. It was the first time she stopped thinking about herself.

"It's Willie," I said. "He's in a real bad way."

"I know," she said. "He comes over here to see me when you're at work."

I was stunned.

"What do you two do?" I asked.

"We sit, mostly."

"Zazen?" I pursued hopefully.

"No. Well, in a way, yes. I sit in zazen and he sits on the sofa drinking and staring off into space."

"I suppose that's something," I mumbled.

"He kind of frightens me, Llew."

"He frightens himself."

"Yeah. That's what I meant. Am I that way?"

I walked over to her and gave her a hug.

"No."

158

She pressed her lips together and looked away. I don't think she believed me.

"Boy, it sure does smell good, whatever you're cooking," I said.

"It's just a stew I threw together. It's ready anytime you are."

"Let me take a shower first, okay?"

"Right." She suddenly called out to me after I was halfway down the hallway. "A letter came for you today. I put in on the bed."

I went into the bedroom, found the letter, and opened it.

Dear Llew,
Socrates once said, "Those who rightly love wisdom are practicing dying." Socrates' death has made me think a lot about dying lately. I have meditated many hours, walked many days on this most important of koans. What could be more important than the question: when I die, what am I? The answer couldn't be simpler: I am something else.
I had to laugh. I knew that. Then I cried for Socrates.
Love,
Zack

Frances approached me from behind.

"Is it anything important?" she asked.

I almost said no. But I changed my mind. I handed her the letter to her surprise. I could tell she read it twice.

"Is Zack a close friend?" she asked.

"Yes."

She looked down at the letter again.

"What's a koan?"

"It's questions and answers."

"I see. And. . .which one is more important?"

"The question is in the answer and the answer is in the question," I said.

"Then one cannot exist without the other."

"That's right. . .and neither one of them exists."

I seemed to reach something within her. She spoke to herself.

"And the answer couldn't be simpler."

She looked at me with a smile. It was the first confident smile I had seen her radiate.

"Yes," I said. "And you've known it all along."

Frances handed the letter back to me and began preparing our cushions for zazen. I was glad, really glad. She got it; whatever it was. She was believing in herself. About what? I wouldn't dare ask. I wouldn't dare hurt the wonderful wave that was going through her.

"Dinner and a shower can wait," she said.

I didn't argue, of course. She had seen something and I simply had to be there with her.

> zen is always here
> and there
> and no where

* * * *

In the last few days, French and Janet had appeared and disappeared like aberrations. They were spending a great deal of time together. In fact, one was not without the other. I was glad that things were changing between them. If for no other reason than that French was trying to take care of Janet. Of course, French had ulterior motives but there was nothing I could do about that. I couldn't deal with Janet and Willie, just Willie. I couldn't deal with Frances and Drew, just Frances. I couldn't deal with work and myself, just work. I suppose one could say that I was kept in a mental haze dealing with Willie and Frances and work. I suppose one could say that I was Willie and Frances and work. There was no reason for me to wonder who I was; no reason at all.

* * * *

Seems like I've been cutting forever, I thought as I drove the riding mower across the edge of a lawn. Frances was getting stronger and Willie was growing weaker. Zazen had been the difference. I knew that. It was only Saturday, the end of a week, yet, the growing strength within Frances had been remarkable. I was happy for Frances and unhappy for Willie. I felt torn, tired, mixed. My feelings conjured up a daydream of Jansen's figure standing before me. He spoke to me in a clear voice.

"Success in one and failure in another. If either one of these penetrates you more than the other, then you are clinging and holding to good and bad; to day and night. If you feel good when you listen to the nice things about you, then you'll feel bad when you listen to the bad things about you. Leave no traces! Answer the next moment without the last. What do you want, Zen?"

* * * *

I waited for Ted to drive away before I began to scan the area more carefully. Willie's car was not in the parking lot of the donut shop. I didn't know whether to be concerned or relieved. I didn't wait. I stopped in at a supermarket and bought a six-pack of beer and a bag of chips on my way home. Willie drove up from behind just as I rounded the final corner which led to my street. He honked his horn and called out to me.

"Hey, where are you going?"

"You were late," I said.

"My damn transmission is slipping. Had a hell of a time getting it into gear."

"You want a beer?"

"I've got a beer. Hop in."

I took my hat off, threw it in the back seat, and got into the car. We drove toward Village Green to a place we called Bush Hill. It was nothing but a mound of dirt created by bulldozers as part of the continuing road construction cutting into the Everglades. Why Bush Hill existed for as many years as it had was anybody's guess. It was an important landmark for many a high school kid: a place to drink, make love, get away. Willie drove to the top of the mound and turned off the car. He stared at the driver's wheel for a long time before he spoke.

"I'm not going to step off a chair."

Willie took a drink from a half-pint of liquor. He seemed to always have a half-pint with him no matter what else there was to drink. The whisky fortified him, strengthened him. He breathed more courageously. He looked at the bottle.

"I can't wait for this to kill me." He looked at me. "Don't be so afraid, Llew."

"If I were brave, I'd have you committed," I said.

"That wouldn't help, my friend. Believe me. I'm too far gone. Reality has no meaning. I won't need a chair."

"Don't do it, Willie. Whatever you're thinking, don't do it.

We're all afraid of life because we know it's a losing battle. The knowledge of this tragedy is what separates us from the rest of the animal kingdom. That we continue to live in the face of this knowledge, in the face of certain defeat, raises us to a level of spiritual nobility."

"If that's what makes men great, I don't want any part of it," Willie flatly stated.

"It's what makes man survive."

"But why?"

"Nobody knows."

Willie's burden returned to his face.

"Wrong answer," he said.

Suddenly, I felt as if I were making a last appeal.

"We must battle heroically against our ultimate conqueror. . . death. Knowing how to do this determines the quality of our life."

Willie was unconvinced.

"Matters of degree in a world without matter," he said. "Each man kills himself in his own way, sooner or later. Can't you feel it? Listen. It's that vague voice we try to ignore. Nobody escapes it. Nobody is entirely free from self-destruction."

"Stop thinking, Willie!"

"And do what!"

I forced myself to calm down.

"Look within yourself," I said.

"That's what I was afraid you'd say," Willie said with a vicious sneer.

He opened the car door, got out, and started walking. I waited for the sound of crunching pebbles to stop before I turned to see where he had gone. He was standing at the edge of the mound. I got out of the car and called out to him.

"Willie. Suicide is an attachment, too!" Willie did not acknowledge me. I should have kept quiet but I didn't. "You're not renouncing anything by killing yourself." I took a few steps toward him and stopped. "True renunciation is the same thing as nonattachment."

Willie squeezed his face together with his hands.

"I don't want the truth; I'm going crazy!" he shouted.

I was scared. Stupid. I should have held my tongue but. . .

"Your mind doesn't matter. What does matter is the nonattachment to the activities of the mind. The picture you have of yourself is killing you. Forget it. Forget yourself!"

"Shut up!"

Willie ran toward me and grabbed the front of my tee shirt. His assault took me off guard. And before I could react, he swung me around and threw me on the ground. He jumped on top of me with the strength of a madman and began choking me as he continued to scream.

"Shut up, shut up, shut up!"

My strength was no match against his and if he hadn't decided to stop, he would have easily killed me. I gasped for air as he went back to his car and started it. But it wouldn't go into gear.

He went into a fitful rage. I believe he actually convulsed.

"I'm going to kill you," he yelled as he started beating and kicking the dashboard of the car. He smashed the gearshift lever with his foot, ending any further hope of driving the car away. "You piece of shit!" He continued to bang and kick and mutilate the Mustang's interior until I thought he was sufficiently exhausted for me to approach him again. By this time, I had recovered from his attack and felt fairly confident that I could handle the situation. I was wrong.

As soon as Willie saw me, he jumped out of the car and transferred his aggressions back to me. I didn't wait. I swung a hard right—my fist connected with his jaw. It was everything I had. And it should have been enough. But it wasn't. Willie was mad. Fortified with madness. He countered with a left jab and a right cut. I went down hard and landed face down on the ground. The heat of the pebbles against my face was the last thing I remembered before the darkness of unconsciousness enveloped me.

* * * *

I traded one kind of darkness for another when I rolled over on my back and opened my eyes. The stars above me were clear and serene. I sat up feeling terrible. I ached to the core. I slowly got up and walked over to the car.

There was no hurry now, I thought.

I was thirsty and hungry and tired so I sat in the front seat, with the car door open, drinking a beer and munching on the chips I had bought earlier. There was nothing else I could do but walk home afterwards.

I forgot my hat.

* * * *

Tommie was back! I was so happy to see him I almost yanked his arm out of joint when we shook hands.

"What happened to you?" he asked.

"Have you seen Willie?"

"No."

"Where's Fran?"

"She's in the kitchen getting dinner ready."

"Fran?" Tommie followed me into the kitchen. "Fran."

"What?" She had the oven door open and was inspecting a roast.

"Have you seen Willie?"

"He didn't stop by today." She looked at me. "What happened to you?"

"Willie's gone crazy."

She closed the oven door and approached me.

"That's a terrible black eye you have." She touched my face. "And that cut needs cleaning."

"Not now." I looked at Tommie. "Help me find Willie?"

"Of course."

Frances pulled her apron off.

"I'm coming," Frances said. I began to protest. "And no arguments."

"Then. . .let's go."

"Where to?" Tommie asked.

"I have no idea," I confessed. "But he's on foot."

"That won't make it any easier," Tommie said.

French and Janet walked through the front door with Tommie's last remark.

"Won't make what easier?" French asked. "What happened to you?"

I looked at Janet.

"It's Willie. He's. . .lost it. I'm really worried about him. We've got to find him."

Janet found it difficult to show any sympathy.

"It won't do any good. Willie's. . .well, he's consumed. But. . . ,"
she looked at French, "we'll help."

"Of course we'll help," French added enthusiastically.
I could tell this was for himself and not Willie. I could tell it
didn't matter one way or the other to Janet. I could tell that Tommie
only had eyes for Frances. I could tell that Frances was going
because of me. I could tell that there was no hope for Willie. I could
tell. . .

Chapter 47
She wasn't listening.

We rode around in French's car until late that night looking for Willie. And when it became apparent to us that it was hopeless, we went for a drive on the freeway.

Nothing feels more desolate than the lights and concrete of a deserted highway. Nothing feels more quiet than the cigarette smoke and silence of a darkened vehicle. Away from the sand and sun, Miami was just another American city: dirty, over-crowded, and bathed in street lights not for illumination but for the protection against crime. Miami always depressed me. There was something unnatural about the way its residential structures had spread in the last ten years, killing everything in sight and destroying what was left of the Everglades.

I leaned my head toward the window and felt the rush of warm air hit my face. It wiped away and clarified my thoughts. I looked up into the expanse of the vast flat sky above and allowed myself to get lost. I closed my eyes, settled comfortably back onto my seat, and crashed and burned into slumber. When I woke up we were pulling up into French's driveway.

Our prevailing silence accompanied us into the house. I felt wide awake now and none of the others would or could go to sleep. But we did split off into private directions. Frances and I went into our bedroom, French and Janet went into the other bedroom, and Tommie remained in the living room.

When I entered the bedroom and shut the door behind me, I suddenly got the sense that this was a last stand for Frances; that she intended to make love with me tonight, or else. So I avoided her by grabbing a set of clean clothes and marching out of there and into the bathroom for a shower as quickly and as inoffensively as I could. It was a childish tactic. But I didn't know what I was doing or what I was trying to prove.

166

Once I was in the shower and had the cool water running, I leaned forward under the spray by supporting myself with both my arms extended in front of me with my palms flat against the tiles on the wall. I let the water beat against the top of my head until I became numb. Then I rinsed my face and stepped out from under the water. When I turned around to reach for the soap I found Frances standing in the bathtub with me. I was too surprised to be startled, too overcome by her naked beauty to be anything but aroused. Neither one of us said a word. What could be said? She stepped closer to me and gave me a kiss. I responded with an embrace that brought our bodies into even closer contact. The delicate softness of her skin and the fiery warmth of her body aroused me so intensely that I had to break away from her.

"I haven't been fair to you, Frances," I said.

"I don't care," she answered.

She knelt down on the tub and attempted to have oral sex with me but I gently resisted and pulled away from her. When I did, the shower drenched her face and hair. She made no attempt to get out from under its trajectory. I knelt down to shield the shower spray with my back. I would have turned it off if I didn't need that sound of running water to fill the void until I could think of something to say. My voice cracked when I finally spoke.

"You want something from me that I cannot give anyone right now."

"We could have made love."

"Then I would have been committed to you in the way you want me to; in the way I'm not capable of. I'm sorry. I've done all the wrong things."

She became angry.

"You're all talk." She struck out at me.

"I like you."

"Yeah, sure."

"In fact, I love you. But not in the way you want me to."

She pushed me away as she stood up.

"Go to hell. My impression of you when we first met was wrong: you're not honest."

She stepped out of the shower, wrapped her bathrobe around her wet body, and slammed the bathroom door shut on her way out. I made no attempt to go after her. I had fallen onto my rear end when she pushed me and there I sat with the shower raining over me. I felt bad and guilty and stupid. I thought of Tommie; the Tommie who probably heard what just happened. Some friend I was. I felt bad and guilty and stupid. I'd hurt Frances. Some friend I was. I stood up and finished my shower. But I could not wash away the web of relationships that were beginning to strangle me into despair. I left my parents' house for the same reasons and now I was going to have to leave here soon. But I had to help Frances in some way before I left.

But Frances was right. I had not been honest. Not with her. Not with myself. Again and again I had denied a commitment that I had made the moment I met her. Over and over I had refused to make a physical commitment, yet willingly encouraged an emotional one, a spiritual one; all along denying the duality of my actions. Had I helped Frances or had I contributed to her problems? Had I been a friend or, in my own way, as destructive to her psychologically as Drew had been physically? I didn't like the questions because suddenly I didn't like the answers that were becoming evident to me.

Chapter 48
"...you can't cry, either."

I didn't bother to go back into the bedroom when I came out of the bathroom. I approached the door, however, and heard the soft painful sounds of weeping. Anything I said to her would have only made it worse.

So, I carefully backed away from the door. And as I passed the other bedroom, I heard the intensity of French and Janet's voices. I stepped closer to their door in order to decipher this intimacy into words.

"What do you see in that creep, Janet?"

"It's what I don't see in you," Janet answered.

A long silence followed.

"I'm sorry, French. I didn't mean to say that."

"What's missing in me? What is there that you don't like about me?"

I heard Janet approach him.

"You're a good man, French. And I wish...I could love you the way you want me to."

French's voice became a little more hopeful.

"Then you do love me, in some way."

"Of course I do. You're a fine person and...and I'm so confused right now. Willie is all the man I can handle right now. I can't be intimate with you anymore. I've tried. But after Willie and me...I'm sorry...don't hate me."

I could tell she was trying to search for the right words; that she was trying to tell French about the malfunctioning sexuality between Willie and her. But she couldn't. Verbalizing it was too much for her. She released an audible gasp of frustration before she finally said, "You just wouldn't understand."

"Why don't you give me a chance?" French stammered belligerently.

"Because I don't understand!" she replied fretfully, emphasizing the personal pronoun, I.

For whatever reasons, French had chosen this moment to discard his seemingly boundless fortitude.

"I hate that bastard for what he has done to you."

"You don't have a right to say that," she countered defensively. "I'm just as much to blame."

French continued to ramble on as if he weren't hearing a word Janet said.

"You dropped out of high school for that bum."

"I was to blame for that. And he's not a bum."

"You left your family because of him."

"They left me. But Mother has come back."

"He took your purity and crushed your soul."

"I've never been a saint. And why would you want damaged goods?"

"He's taken everything from you."

"Then what do you see in me that's left? What do you want from me? Or is it, what do you want to make of me? French. Look at me. French! You're not listening."

"I hate him," he whispered.

A short reticence followed before Janet spoke.

"You and I, French. . .I don't think so."

"Where are you going?"

"To pack my things."

"But you can't go now."

"You don't want me. You want Willie's girl. My God, I don't exist! I've got to get out of here; I'm suffocating."

I stepped away from the door anticipating her departure; it remained closed. I approached the door again after allowing a few moments to pass.

"Take your hands off of me, French."

"You've got to listen to me, Janet."

"I'm through listening. I've. . .take. . .your. . ." I heard the sound of a slap followed by a long dispersal of silence. Janet was calm but relentless. "I may as well have stayed with Willie."

The remark had been directed by Janet to hurt him; that she had succeeded so completely was her only miscalculation. I heard French walk away from her. He threw himself on the bed and began to cry into a pillow.

"Oh, God, French, I didn't mean that."

French managed to stop crying long enough to say, "But you're right. I'm no better. I'm. . ."

He resumed sobbing.

I heard her go to the bed and sit beside him.

"Stop it, French. Stop it," she said. "If I can't cry, you can't cry, either."

Silence followed; a kind of silence that said more than a thousand words.

"Do you know where my Mom lives?" she asked.

"Of course," French answered.

"Would you take me home?"

"Yeah, in a minute, okay?"

"Okay."

I backed away from their door and traveled up the hallway into the living room where Tommie was waiting. He was a mess.

"What's happening in there? Are they going to be alright?"

"Maybe," I said.

"Does that go for me, too?"

"I guess you heard what happened in the bathroom."

Tommie could only nod his head, yes.

"Can I borrow your car?" I continued.

"Sure."

He freely handed me his keys.

"I'm going out again to look for Willie."

"What about Frances?"

"She could use your help." Tommie didn't know how to answer me.

"But she doesn't want my help."

"Open the door, walk in, and be yourself. It would be more than I've done."

He walked past me toward the hallway as if he were approaching a gallows.

"Yeah, be myself," he said. "Easy for you to say."

I think I smiled.

"Good luck."

I left him standing there not knowing if he would actually go in to see her or not. Then I got into his car and drove away not thinking about anything; not even thinking about Willie.

Chapter 49
Intermezzo

Catherine welcomed all hobos at our door. 921 was located near a defunct railroad station. They offered to work for their keep but refused money. They would say, "I'd only buy the devil's brew with it ma'am. I need to eat something."

So, she'd disappear for a few moments, leaving them stand on the porch with their hat in hand and gingerly looking through the screen door with anticipation. When she'd reappear, they would break out into a thankful smile and step away from the door.

She'd step out onto the porch and dominate the space with her small frame before handing them a can of soup and a piece of bread. They reflected her kind gentleness in the way they accepted their alms. Then they would bow in obeisance to her as if she were a saint; she didn't understand holiness. Her heart simply operated in a compassionate manner. They knew this and never took advantage of her. I know this for a fact because they never returned for more food.

> Two stars, a pair
> they must be her eyes. . .
> Two curls, a mouth
> this must be a smile. . .

Chapter 50
Leftover Raindrops

My eyes burned with fatigue as I sat in the car in front of French's house and waited for the rain to stop. I had been up all night combing the streets of South Miami looking for Willie. It was long past sunrise and the sun seemed to shoot up into the sky rather than rise like a heavenly body. I was able to roll down the window on my side about halfway because of the way the rain slanted from the other direction. I gazed out through the opened window and scanned the neighborhood, but I could not forget my discomfort.

The rain is not cool in the summer, not in Miami. The rain is wet and as heavy as the onslaught of humidity which follows immediately after a shower. The glistening streets turn into saunas with the aid of a cloudless sky and a relentless sun. Even if shade can be found, it is useless against the effects of what the natives call a "sun shower."

And within half an hour, all the evidence of this rain will completely disappear. The intensity of the sun will bleach the stucco homes bone white again and bear down cruelly upon the remaining colors exposed to its rays; in a few short years, this kind of abuse will fade and burn these primary pigments closer to pastels.

The rain stopped as abruptly as it started, leaving behind the short life span of a leaking world. I looked through the windshield and focused upon the rural mailbox that was approximately four feet dead ahead. On a hunch, I got out of the car and walked over to the mailbox. I had this feeling that French had forgotten to check the mail yesterday. When I opened it, I discovered a single letter addressed to me. It was from Zack. I carefully tore open the envelope and unfolded the letter.

Dear Llew,

I made these decisions right after I sent my last letter to you this morning. Had to write you again.

By the time you receive this, I'll have left the YMCA and have returned to the streets of Baltimore. Don't ask me why because I'm going to tell you. Socrates isn't the only person who has died. Largo has died, too. He was murdered for no apparent reason the other night while asleep in an alley. Sorry. I almost couldn't tell you.

I must go back out there and take his place. Call it the ritual of death Largo deserves. It will be my contribution toward the erasure of his karma. And even though everyone's karma is his own, to be changed by his own will, it is believed that once created it becomes all and everyone's; affecting everyone. Knowing that, there is hope for eliminating all suffering. I know. This is all very Buddhistic. I'm sorry.

I'll end this letter by saying I desire nothing from Largo. Don't think of me. Think of yourself until you see me and forget the self. Don't bother to write. Your letter won't find me.

     Fish sends love

     Zack

I read the letter a second time before going back to Tommie's car. I was stunned. I got back inside and rummaged through his glove compartment until I found a pack of matches. I struck a match and lit the corner of the letter and the envelope and watched the flame grow. The fire consumed Largo just as it consumed Jansen when we cremated him in the Shenandoah Valley. It was about the same time of day when Zack, Fish, Largo, and I stood around his burning bier feeding the flame with the wood we had gathered. I remembered the heat of the fire warmed us from the bitter cold of winter. Still, it was cold now; a different kind of cold that comes from being alone during a time like this. This was a gesture, a trifle. But it was what I could do; that. . . and my silent tears.

The flame began to subside, leaving a large delicate ash threatening to crumble into a million fragments. When the flame died to a slow ember about an inch from my finger, I stuck my arm out the window and let the remains blow away with a rare gust of wind.

I remained in my seat staring through a windshield pocked with beads of leftover raindrops. I was frozen in time: seeing my own death, seeing my own life in the present. I wiped away the two streams of tears from my cheeks with my hands. Then childish thoughts came to my rescue; poetic thoughts with their quiet touch:

I understand! I understand! loving. . .
I understand the moisture of the earth
I understand the sweet caress of the living
by the sorrows of animals and man.

I see the burden of our touching
I see the burden of being touched
I see the burden of having been touched
by someone or something, that someday
will cease to exist.

So I cry for the future that is mine
And I cry for that future beyond my life
I cry for the future that lies before us all
I cry and I cry for this life of pain,
this life of suffering
this life of the ordinary with its quiet touch
of death.

Chapter 51
Guilt

I had to go to the bathroom. I hopped out of Tommie's car and as I started for the house, I realized that French's car was not parked in the driveway. The prevailing stillness that surrounded me when I entered the house confirmed that nobody was home. I felt a sudden sense of foreboding as I walked toward the bathroom to answer the call of nature; this sense was not without cause.

I stopped in front of the opened doorway mesmerized by the inanimate object that used to be Willie. His grotesque figure hung lifelessly by the leather belt he had looped around his neck before tying the other end to the shower head. The fact that the shower head was not tall enough did not deter Willie's resolve to end his life in this way. He simply raised his feet by bending his legs at the knees and held them up by reaching behind himself with both arms and grasping his ankles, one in each hand. That he managed to hold himself in that position of death was a testament to his superhuman determination. This scene was so odd, so impossible, that I dared not destroy the composition. I feared that the police wouldn't believe this unless they saw it for themselves.

I staggered forward instead of backward, into instead of out of the bathroom. I had to approach him. I had to say something. But all that came out of me was a lame apology.

"God, Willie, I'm sorry."

His tongue was swollen, his facial features bluish black and his opened eyes bulged hideously upward. I had to turn away. I had to urinate.

After I relieved myself, I happened to look down into the bathtub. A torn, half sheet of paper caught my eye. I reached down, picked it up and read it.

Janet,
I wanted to kill you.
So, I murdered myself.
I'm no longer guilty.
Forgive me.
Will

I shuddered. I found it hard to think. I looked at him. There was no use judging Willie's twisted thoughts. I tried not to while he was alive; there was no use doing so now that he was dead. I flushed the toilet and walked out of the bathroom. The note was still in my hand when French and Tommie walked into the living room.

"Man, where have you been?" French inquired.

"We've been looking for you all night," Tommie added.

I handed Willie's suicide note to French. He looked at it rather dumbly before he read it and handed it to Tommie.

"What's this supposed to mean?" French asked.

"Willie's dead," I answered.

"What? Where is he?"

"In the bathroom," I said. And as they both started for the bathroom, I added, "Don't go in there."

Neither one of them listened. I heard Tommie's vocal exclamation first.

"Jesus Christ! He hanged himself!"

"My God, look at that!" was what French managed to say before they both tumbled out of the bathroom and back to me in the living room.

"What the hell happened?" Tommie demanded.

"I don't know," I said.

Tommie shuddered in much the same way I had.

"Did you see that?" he said to me. "It gives me the creeps."

French looked pale. Almost sick.

"Are you alright, French?" I asked.

Tommie caught him by the arm and led him to the sofa where he sat down. I knelt down in front of him and waited until he was able to speak while Tommie quietly sat down beside French. When French was ready to speak he looked directly at me.

"I feel guilty," he said. I didn't ask why. "I'm glad he's dead."

"Because of Janet?" Tommie whispered understandingly.

French's eyes widened.

"Yes. I hated the bastard. He was ugly to Janet. He used her. I love her. I always have."

French buried his face into his hands.

I didn't know what to say to him. I looked at Tommie and could tell he didn't know what to say either. French finally dropped his hands away from his face. And when he raised his head, the astonishment of Willie's suicide was still painted across his countenance.

"He killed himself," French stated once again as if it were a newly discovered secret. He was suffering from a mild form of shock. I touched him on the shoulder affectionately.

"It doesn't matter now, French."

"That's right," Tommie added. "There's nothing we can do now."

There was no use going into the details of Willie's suffering, I thought. Besides, I really didn't understand them myself. I failed him, though. We all failed him. I felt. . .inadequate.

"It does matter," French finally decided.

"Okay," I said without resistance.

"And I feel so bad. I feel like—"

"It's not your fault," I said firmly. "Willie began to commit suicide long before he became. . ." I was going to say "impotent" but I decided there was no use going into that. "Long before he looped his belt around his neck; long before he tied the other end over the shower head; long before he raised his feet and held them up in the air with his hands. No. There's no reason to feel guilty, French." I didn't bother to say that it was everybody's fault. I didn't bother to say that there was no such thing as fault. But there was fault in the world. It did exist. So, where was this no-fault that Jansen had spoken about? To what plane of existence was he referring? There were still so many questions. Where were the answers?

"There can never be anything between me and Janet after all this," French declared somberly.

French was thinking about French. My hand dropped from his shoulder without judgment.

"Where is Janet?" I asked.

"We dropped her off at her Mom's house in North Miami," Tommie said.

"Somebody needs to tell her before we call the police," I said.

"I'll take care of it," French said as he endeavored to crawl out of his slump.

"Where's Fran?" I finally asked.

"She's gone," French answered.

I looked at Tommie. He had become visibly agitated.

"I went with French to take Janet to her Mom's after you left. I just didn't have the guts to approach Frances. You know how I am. I rode along just to get out of the house. When we got back here, I got this funny feeling that Frances was gone. The house felt empty; I don't know. When I checked the bedroom I found this."

Tommie stood up and reached into his pocket. He pulled out a crumpled piece of paper that had been folded several times and handed it to me.

"She left you this."

I unfolded the paper and read the note.

> Llew,
> Have gone back to Drew.
> Stay away. I don't want
> anybody getting hurt.
> Fran

I looked at Tommie. He shrugged his shoulders.

"Like I said, we've been trying to find you all night," he said. "We rode all over South Miami looking for you.

"She's crazy, Tom. That Drew character will hurt her. Maybe even. . .can I use your car again?"

"I'll take you there," he said. "If I'm ever going to mean anything to her, I've got to be there."

Fran's note was still in my hand; Willie's note was still in Tommie's hand. "I don't think Janet needs to read this, do you?"

"No," French interjected.

I still had the pack of matches I found in the glove compartment of Tommie's car. I took the pack out of my pocket, struck a match, and lit Fran's note first.

"This one may as well go, too," I said.

Tommie agreed by touching Willie's note against the flame of Fran's note.

"Are you going to be able to handle telling Janet and calling the police?" I asked French.

"Yes," he answered as he stood up with determination. French had regained control of himself again with his eyes reflecting his full composure. He picked up an ashtray from a side table and offered it to Tommie. Tommie deposited what was left of Willie's burning note into it and passed the ashtray to me. When I dropped Fran's burning note into the ashtray, French reached out for it.

"I'll flush this down the toilet," he said as I handed it to him.

I looked at Tommie.

"Are you ready?"

"Yeah."

"Then come on," I said.

We left French behind to call Janet and the police. There was no reason to say anything else. All of us were facing something we did not want to do. More words would have made our tasks more difficult; more words would have confused us, more or less. . .into immobility.

> Where does the pain go?
> Saddened as I look away. . .
> Dead cat on the road

Chapter 52
I was no longer there.

Tommie drove. And since he remembered where Drew's house was located, neither one of us said anything until we were almost there.

"Third house on the left," he said.

"That's right," I confirmed.

Tommie nodded rather grimly. The tone in my voice must have reflected my recollection of Fran's environment. I looked at the house as we braked momentarily in front of the place with the car still running. Now that I was aware of the condition of its interior, the exterior of the single-story, white stucco structure appeared to be just as wretched.

Chickweed, stickers, crab grass, and dandelions dominated the lawn that surrounded the house. Mildew crept up the walls from the ground below, surrounding the house with a jagged green border three times the height of most interior floorboards. A matching border of black crud and rust leaked from behind corroded gutters and stained the soffits, the eaves, and the upper portion of the white stucco wall with a dark brown mold.

"Looks pretty depressing, doesn't it?" Tommie said.

"Don't worry," I said. "We'll get her out of there."

"But will we get that out of her?"

"That's your job, remember?"

"Yeah," Tommie answered after he let his foot off the brake. "I'm willing."

He parked the car in front of the house on the opposite side of the street. And as we crossed the street and made our final approach, I noted that there were very few cars left in the neighborhood. It was morning and everybody had already left for work.

"That guy, Drew, his car is not here," I noted aloud.

"I hope Frances is alone."

"She may not have been last night," I cautioned.

"I don't care," Tommie insisted as he forced the thought out of his mind at the same time.

I wanted to make sure he was going into this thing with his eyes wide open. Frances had problems. They were going to be his problems until they could work things out together.

Tommie looked at me as if he were reading my mind.

"Don't worry, Llew. I know what's going on. I know what I'm doing."

"Then everything's going to be alright. Frances is a good person. She's just—"

"I know. . .I know."

We walked right in; the front door was unlocked.

The interior had only marginally improved in appearance and stench. There were a few plastic trash bags filled with some of the garbage that had been piled up against the wall. And some of the cigarette butts and broken glass on the floor had been swept into several small piles.

Frances was startled when she walked into the living room and discovered our presence. She was carrying a foxtail brush and a dustpan. Her face blanched with despair.

". . .trying to clean this place up." She turned away from us. "I told you not to come."

"You never said anything about me," Tommie asserted.

She did not acknowledge Tommie. She kept her back to both of us.

"I tried, Llew. But I can't live like you. I can't believe in that stuff. . .that—"

"I don't want you to believe in anything." I said. "All I wanted you to do was sit; and see for yourself."

She did not acknowledge me this time.

"Why do you keep coming back to this creep?" Tommie boldly asked. "Are you nuts?"

Frances turned around and faced us.

"Yes," she said as she tossed the foxtail and dustpan onto the sofa. "I'm sorry. I can't. . .I. . . ." She began to cry. Tommie walked over to her and tried to comfort her with a caress. She did not physically resist. Instead, she looked at Tommie and said, "Please, get out of here before both of you get hurt. Drew's got a gun with him."

"Where is he?" I asked.

Her gaze remained firmly planted on Tommie.

"He and Mark went out to get sausage biscuits. They're going to be home any minute now."

"Home?" Tommie responded incredulously. "You call this insane asylum home?"

"It's all I have," she said.

"Me!" Tommie said firmly. "You've got me!" His voice trembled to a whisper. "If you want me."

She stammered.

"Why would you. . .I mean. . .I. . ."

"I need you," Tommie declared. "And you need me."

They continued to talk. I was no longer there. I watched as they finally stepped into each other's lives with wide open eyes. It was a relief to see the element of genuine concern openly develop between them. For a few brief moments they had forgotten their surroundings, their predicament, themselves. Maybe this was not a prelude to love but it was genuine human contact, genuine reaching.

I stepped toward a window and posted myself as a lookout to give them as much time to establish themselves with each other as possible. I was happy to be able to listen to a crystallization of hope between them. It wasn't much; she needed real help; but it would have to do for now. Because Drew and Mark pulled up into the driveway.

"They're here," I announced. "Get out of here."

"Is there a back door?" Tommie asked.

"Yes, through the kitchen," Frances answered apprehensively.

"Okay, let's go," I said.

The back door was in the kitchen. And as soon as Frances and Tommie stepped over its threshold, I swung the door closed and locked them out. Tommie tried opening the door.

"What the hell do you think you're doing?" Tommie demanded.

"Don't be stupid," Frances declared.

"Do you want them to come after you?" I said. "Eventually, they would. You know that. Can you deny that was at least part of the reason you came back?"

"No," she finally stated with determination.

"Then I'm going to stay here and finish this; make sure they never come looking for you again; make sure you'll never dare want to return here again no matter how afraid you become." Another silence followed. "Frances. I've never meant to hurt you. I hope you understand. . ."

"Yes," she interjected. "I understand. But. . .why? Why you? Why must you do this?" she asked softly.

"Because I'm here. . .and. . .in my own way I love you," I said. "And I'm sorry if that doesn't make any sense." I heard Drew and Mark at the front door. "Now get out of here," I said gruffly.

"Come on, Frances," Tommie urged. And as soon as I heard them walk away, I turned around and walked into the living room. Mark cackled loudly at Drew as soon as he saw me.

"I knew he was here. I told you that was their car."

Now I knew why it took them so long to come in. They had been deliberating about our. . .my presence.

"Where's Frances?" Drew demanded, as he dropped a small bag of sausage biscuits on the floor.

"Gone," I said.

"Jesus Christ. You goodie-two-shoes never fuckin' learn. She's a dumb whore. Tell him, Mark."

"You shoulda seen what we did to her last night," Mark grinned, showing his broken teeth.

"That's none of my business," I said.

"Yeah," Drew uttered. "We shoulda gotten it on tape. It would've been a real triple-ecstasy film."

I decided I may as well piss them off and get this over with.

"You're a couple of real scum bags."

Mark flipped his knife out as an immediate response to my derogatory remark.

"Well, scum this, jerk bag. I'm going to cut you up into little pieces."

Drew pulled out a revolver and pointed it at me.

"And you're going to let him do it," Drew said.

Mark cackled hysterically.

"I love it when things are going our way!"

My eyes reflected death. . .my death. . .our death.

Mark took a step toward me.

"Watch it, Mark," Drew cautioned.

"What!" Mark answered, sensing Drew's apprehension.

"He's not afraid, man, be careful."

Mark looked into my eyes as Drew had apparently done. He wasn't quite so sure of himself anymore. He hesitated. "You and your big mouth," Mark said. "Use your damn gun if you have to."

I circled around toward my right, placing Mark between me and Drew. When Mark realized what I had done, he scurried a little toward his left.

"Hey. . .hey," Mark explosively demanded.

"What!" Drew snapped.

"Be careful you don't shoot me, now," Mark urged.

"I'm not stupid!" Drew rebutted excitedly.

Mark backed away from me and directed himself toward Drew until he stood beside him. It was like a stalemate.

"Ah hell, shoot the bastard, Drew."

Drew nervously licked the rim of his mouth. Beads of sweat appeared on his upper lip and his dark eyes became darker.

"What are you waiting for?" Mark prodded.

Drew ran his free hand through his very dirty long blond hair. Mark began to flush red with anger. His short red hair seemed to stand straight up like half a dozen pencil strokes representing hair on a stick figure. Mark reached for the revolver.

"Give me that damn thing," Mark ordered.

Drew pushed him away as he said, "No."

Mark reacted like a viper and struck out at Drew with his knife. He slashed his forearm without thinking, causing blood to flow. When Drew grabbed his forearm in response to his wound, Mark reached for the revolver again. This time he managed to get hold of it but Drew would not release his grip. They struggled for its possession until they managed to accidently fire the revolver. The bullet bit into Mark's thigh, leaving behind a superficial gash which bled profusely. Mark screamed as he released the weapon and clutched his left thigh. He hopped around the living room agonizing over the pain.

"You son of a bitch! I'm gonna kill you!"

"Hey man, I'm sorry," Drew said. "You shouldn't have. . ."

Then he suddenly remembered his forearm and presented it to him.

"And what about this!"

"I'm sorry, I'm sorry, I got mad. But you didn't have to shoot me!"

"You shot yourself, you dumb bastard."

They were both bleeding excessively. So, I started walking toward the kitchen thinking that they almost would have been humorous if they weren't so pitiful.

"Where the hell do you think you're going?" Mark challenged.

"To find something clean to put on those wounds, you dumb jerk."

Both their faces flattened into a stupid looking bewilderment. Drew actually pointed his revolver casually toward another direction.

"There are a few towels in the bathroom," he lamely suggested.

"That'll do," I said.

I left the two of them meandering in the living room and cursing each other for the injuries they had inflicted upon each other. Once I was out of their sight, I had to laugh. This was insanity!

I returned with two marginally clean towels and used them to apply direct pressure on their wounds. Mark sat on the sofa while Drew remained standing. They looked like a pair of injured mongrels. As I took another look at Mark's thigh to make sure he had the bleeding under control, Drew suddenly became suspicious.

"Man, what is it with you?"

I looked up at him. But before I could say anything, Mark reversed the challenge back to Drew.

"What is it with you? First, you won't shoot him. Then, you shoot me! Something's wrong with this picture."

"Shut up," Drew countered with self-contempt as he finally put the revolver back into his right rear pocket.

Upon seeing that, Mark simply stabbed the knife into the main cushion of the sofa and left it there, buried to the hilt. It more or less symbolized their defeat.

"Are you two going to be alright?" I asked.

"Yeah, yeah," Drew snapped irritably.

"Then I think I'll go now," I added.

Mark managed to express the ironic situation with one final laconic statement.

"Hell, it seems like you can do whatever you want around here."

I checked myself as I started to leave.

"And one more thing," I said. They both looked at me. "Frances is not coming back here. Do the both of you understand that?"

Drew responded with a ruined nod. Mark took the easier way out by not responding at all. Neither of them had the will to challenge me.

I walked through the front door and found Tommie and Frances waiting for me. I smiled even though I felt ashamed.

"I saw everything through the window," Tommie said. "Glad things worked out."

"We weren't sure what we were going to do, but we weren't going to leave you alone," Frances calmly stated.

I looked at Frances.

"I'm not going to be mad at you," Frances said. "I'm sick and tired of being angry and scared." She looked at Tommie. "Let's get out of here."

They got into the car and when they realized I wasn't getting in with them, Tommie called out, "Hey, aren't you coming?"

"No," I said. "I need to be alone."

"Are you going to be alright?" Frances asked.

"Sure. Are you going back to French's house?"

"Where else?" she answered.

"I'll meet you. . .both there, later. Okay?"

I looked away from Frances, momentarily.

"Sure," she said. "Okay. Just. . .be careful, alright?"

Tommie started the car and began to drive away. And when I looked back at Frances, I saw a kind smile on her face that remained focused upon me until the car turned the corner and disappeared.

I felt empty and incomplete and it was nothing but my own fault. I started walking in the opposite direction.

Chapter 53
Intermezzo

We met in Okinawa. His name was Vero Siento; an Italian from New York City. I didn't like him much. He was a phony: he acted like a tough guy but he wore his fear on his sleeves; he boasted about his physical prowess but he was out of shape and sloppy. He was a phony. But we were both heading for Vietnam. I welcomed all friendships.

He liked to drink scotch and milk. So, I got drunk with him on scotch and milk for the first and only time in my life, in my first and only night in Okinawa. I was glad I did this.

Vero was killed in action nine months later. He was posthumously awarded the Silver Star and the Navy Cross Medals for valor in combat against the enemy. He was a hero.

    nothing
    more noble than
    the innocence of going to war
    the innocence of a thirty day leave
    the innocence of anticipation:
    looking forward to leaving home
    again, not knowing where
    one is going or what one may be doing

    nothing
    more noble than
    arriving in a strange land
    arriving among the trembling
    arriving with naked innocence:
    looking outward instead of inward
    again, eyes disappearing where
    the subject becomes the object

nothing
more noble than
the fear of discovering war
the fear of being   found out
the fear of mortality arriving:
looking toward others for identity
again, discovering the self where
the self has always been

nothing
more noble than
crying out with horror
crying out for the dead   inside
crying out because of fear:
looking inward for the first time
again, realizing a mistake where
stillness might have prevented it all

nothing
more noble than
giving up your life for another
giving up all hope of becoming   someone else
giving up crying:
looking nowhere for that fatal bullet
again, understanding life could still end where
ever thoughts begin to separate one from another

nothing
more noble than
hunger for cleanliness in the mud
hunger for the four noble truths
hunger for the pleasure of forgiving:
looking for nothing in return
again, the simplicity of life is located where
the source of life is generated by a pulse

nothing
more noble than
sharing one's dream with another toy soldier
sharing one's food with a peasant Tom Sawyer
sharing in the eternal wish that is everyone's hunger:
looking forward to a future
again, when all war can be where
all wars should be   over

Chapter 54
I felt empty.

"Hello, French? It's me."

"Where are you, Llew?"

"I'm at a telephone booth near the Royal Castle on Bird Road and 107th Avenue. Are Tom and Frances there?"

"Yeah."

"Did they tell you what happened?"

"What do you think?"

"Then you know Drew and Mark won't give them any more trouble."

"Were you hurt?"

"Hell, French, who hasn't been hurt in the last twenty-four hours? What about Willie?"

"The police and the paramedics are still here. The incident, as they call it, appears to be routine."

"I see. Are you alright?"

"What's alright, Llew?"

"I know. . .Janet. Did you tell her about Willie?"

"I had to. But I'm sorry I did."

"Why?"

"She was cold. Real cold. She didn't shed a tear."

I pressed my forehead against the pay telephone.

"Don't expect too much from her, French."

He responded to me as if he hadn't been listening.

"I offered to take her to the coroner. She actually wants to go."

"Give her room. She's suffocating."

"Who's fault is that?"

"Nobody's. French. . .she needs you more than ever."

"You think so?"

"Give her time."

I heard somebody interrupt him.

"Tom wants to talk to you."

"Put him on."

Tommie was glowing. He whispered to me: "Frances cried on my shoulder. She was sad about Willie and happy about us. It's crazy, isn't it?" He handed the telephone back to French without waiting for my response. Then I told French that I would be at his place the following morning to pack my bags and bid them farewell before I left town. He made no attempt to change my mind.

I hung up the telephone, then immediately lifted it off the hook again. I felt empty.

I deposited fifteen cents in the change receiver and dialed my parents' number. As I listened to the telephone ring, I suddenly felt a little guilty. I needed to apologize to them for not keeping in touch. But when my mother answered the telephone and discovered that it was me, I realized that an apology was not necessary. The tone of her voice was gentle.

"Sure, I'm alright. How are you, Mom? I'm glad. And Pop? Good. I love you both, you know that.

"No. There's no reason for my call. I simply wanted to know how both of you were doing. No, I don't need any money, thanks. Don't worry, I'm fine. Tell Pop. . .give him a kiss for me when he gets home, okay? I love you too. Bye."

During the silence that followed, I hung up the telephone. I felt empty.

I stared at the telephone's change box. Upon its chrome plating, my reflection was a blur.

Chapter 55
Intermezzo

I have often dwelled upon the early portion of our marriage because we never graduated to that level where two people begin to take each other for granted.

We never forgot to be polite to each other or to be respectful of one another's privacy. Throughout the years of our marriage, we gave each other space to move around in.

We always had each other's welfare in mind and were always proud of each other's achievements. We truly stood side by side as equals, careful not to place too many personal demands on the other; the ultimate gesture of love and respect.

All the more reason for my disorientation after her death. All the more reason for my incapacitating suffering which followed. In the wake of losing her, I lost my home, my ambition, my career, and my self.

Ephemeral. Throughout every day of our lives together, I knew it was all ephemeral. I thought this was some kind of strength. I even thought this was knowledge. It wasn't.

It didn't matter that, after the war, I considered the rest of my life a gift. It didn't matter that I could look back and say that I appreciated every moment I had with Catherine. This was not knowledge.

Our years of marriage were complete, untarnished. . .and over. And like the war, this too would be a part of my life played over and over.

Does anything ever really die? I don't know. But I would like to wish, even though I don't believe in wishing, for one more kiss, for one more tangible embrace from my Catherine. But what is tangible? And what is knowledge?

I'm not Llewellen. And I'm not Jansen.

forever knowing my weaknesses
forever seeing them in the darkness
  of a slumberless night

restless within a chink of a night light
and listening to the distance of barking dogs

finding myself lost; once again
looking for things
that have always been there

where? are these thoughts leading
where? did they come from in the first place—

filled with illusions
filled with the darkness
  and a chink of light

Chapter 56
Another Slumber

I decided to have a cup of coffee before I did anything else. So I walked into the Royal Castle. It was like a freezer in there with the air conditioning turned down so low. I noticed that drops of condensation had formed on the lower halves of the plate glass windows which served as three of the building's outer walls. A lady, about my age, was working alone. She was plain, clean, wore kitchen white, and knew how to be quietly pleasant to a customer. I sat down at the counter and ordered coffee. When she placed the cup in front of me, she offered no conversation, no cream, and no sugar. She went about her business preparing for the breakfast crowd as if I weren't there. I was grateful.

I sipped my coffee and wondered why I was going to miss Ted so much.

I drank two more cups of coffee without being able to answer this question, left a dollar on the counter, and walked out.

I hitchhiked all the way down Bird Road to Dixie Highway, then walked the rest of the way to Coconut Grove Bayfront Park to spend the rest of the day and night there. It was almost a pleasant day, for Miami; the heat was not too unbearable. I walked around the park's surrounding district and happened across a small used-book store. They were one of my favorite kinds of places. So, I decided to go in and browse around. The store's shelves were pleasantly over-stocked with books that had been shelved according to subject category. Only the fiction section was alphabetized by author.

The lady behind a small counter looked up momentarily from a book she was reading to see who it was. She reciprocated a smile, then returned to her book without concern. She didn't bother to ask me if I needed help.

I walked down several aisles of books until I happened across the Religion and Philosophy section. For some reason, a small green paperback book caught my eye. So I pulled it off the shelf and read the title, *The Lankavatara Sutra*. I opened the book and discovered, after reading the Introduction, that this was one of the key scriptures of Mahayana Buddhism and one of the most influential of the Zen sect. I also discovered that Bodhidharma, the founder of Zen, once said that this was the only sutra one needed to study. I randomly flipped to a page toward the center of the book and began to read. For some unknown reason, I read the passage to myself, aloud.

"The Blessed one (Buddha) contemplated stillness and therefore left behind birth and death. This is called non-attachment. No one has ever become Buddha (Awakened) without sitting in meditation."

I started flipping through the pages again and when I reached the end of the book, I discovered a brochure tucked between the last page and the back cover. It was a single sheet of buff-colored paper folded in thirds. On the front was a picture of a group of people sitting in zazen. The composition captured my attention for a long time; the environment and the people within it appeared quite serene. Then I turned to the back of the brochure and noted a daily training schedule: from wake-up to lights-out. The structure of the training appeared no less rigorous than that of a military boot camp. That fascinated me. I understood boot camps. I noted periods of zazen, meals, work, classes, services, interviews, and rest periods. There was structure. There were rules. All apparently necessary to create an environment that helped in maintaining freedom from distractions. And, of course, since this was a monastery, the point of this freedom was to help deepen spiritual training.

I opened up the brochure and I was captivated by the small photographs inside: the simplicity and cleanliness of the grounds, the quiet and demanding structure of daily life, and finally, the serene yet determined faces of the people.

I noted information such as registration and fees, Introductory Retreats and Resident Lay Training Programs. But I came to a stop when I read about the availability of positions for full-time Resident Student-Monks, similar to a college work-study program. With my limited funds, I knew that was the way I would have to go. I did have enough money to pay for a few weeks of residency and that would get me in. Once they saw my determination, my hard work and dedication, how could they refuse my application for residency?

Suddenly, I realized what I was saying to myself; what I was committing myself to; what I was thinking here. Did I really want to go to a monastery? (I looked at the front cover again.) To this Mountain Echo Monastery? I paused momentarily. Then I knew the answer was yes.

I began to smile. I had a purpose. Suddenly. Decisively. I had a direction. I'd discovered a method to pursue Jansen's Buddhistic idealogy. I saw a way to find out just how or where I had gone wrong. I saw a way to find out if I was even on the right path! Had Jansen been real? Had I understood anything he taught me? I had to find out, once and for all. I had to go to California, to this Mountain Echo Monastery. My sense of failure and the weight of my thoughts pressing in on me were no longer as severe. I now saw hope in the horizon; no, more than that: I saw the possible end of chaos and indecision in my life, once and for all. Instinctively, I knew that whether I embraced the Zen life at this monastery or not, I was finally going to fully embrace life; and, in fact, escape into it. . .whatever that was. . .once and for all.

I was able to spend a few hours reading the sutra within the cool shadows of the bookstore without many suspicious glances from the clerk. When I was sure I had worn out my welcome, I paid for the book and left.

I walked straight to the park and enjoyed the latter part of the day. I had a fine book under my arm, money in my pocket, and time to blow away. When I got hungry, I bought a couple of hot dogs from a street vendor. When I got thirsty, I drank from the park's water fountain. What could be simpler?

By nightfall, I was far from being alone. It seemed like the later it got, the more people arrived at the park. It was actually crowded and noisy and busy with activity.

It was very late before I was able to find a place to hide and sleep without being disturbed by the police. During the course of the evening, I had drunk several beers and eaten another hot dog. I even managed to prevent further direct contact with people.

When I lay down behind the clump of bushes I had chosen, I

suddenly realized that I was exhausted. I hadn't slept the night before and the emotional strain of Willie's and Largo's deaths, of Janet and French, of Frances and Tommie, of Drew and Mark, and of Mom and Dad had finally taken its toll on me. My eyes burned when I closed them and my body spun with fatigue as I lay there on my back. An unexpected pang of guilt stabbed at my heart over my failure with Willie. It was my last conscious thought; I didn't remember falling asleep; I didn't remember the beginning of my dream. That is, if hearing Jansen's voice was a dream. He spoke softly to me:

"You think you may have failed, but you have not. You have to learn to deal with yourself first. You have to solve your own problems before you can help and teach others. You have to learn and practice very hard. Years. Whatever it takes. Forget about going out into the world. Become whole and awakened first. Understand the nature of yourself and the world; these are not separate. When you do this, then your help will have meaning, have impact, have value, but most important of all. . .have compassion. Taking action too soon is dangerous without this compassion. This doesn't mean that you won't fail or make mistakes. That is a part of being successful and making the right decisions. Black and white, right or wrong, is the emptiness at the center of the wheel. Without this emptiness in the middle, the wheel cannot turn."

I woke up in the middle of the night. I don't know why I was startled. My eyes were wide-open but unfocused. I sat up and rubbed them. And after I blinked my eyes a couple of times, I saw Jansen. He was standing over me. Clearly. Completely. Was he really there? This was not a dream. I knew that. Because the things he said to me were not a recollection. This was not something Jansen had once told me when he was alive. Nor was this something I had projected into Jansen in a daydream. This was Jansen! Flesh and blood. He was not wearing his peacoat or sweater or woolen watch cap; this was not Baltimore. He wore the uniform of the day: blue jeans and a tee shirt. His face was bright and his dark eyes glowed. His dark hair had been cut shorter, his face had been shaved, and his fair skin had a slight tan. This was Jansen but. . .but he had changed. I was almost frightened. But as soon as Jansen began to speak, I forgot my fear.

"This is the last time I am going to speak to you. I exist but you must forget me. You will not be able to see your own existence until you erase the cloud of mine. There have been too many words between us. That is my fault. Bodhidharma, the first Zen patriarch, emphasized mind-to-mind transmission because words are another attachment; a verbal entanglement. But don't forget, he did not reject the sutras and the sastras."

I looked at my paperback book lying beside me. Jansen didn't seem to take notice. He continued to speak.

"Study the scriptures. It will give you confidence. Most of all, and I know you know this, practice. . .practice your zazen daily. . .practice often. . .practice with as many people as you can. And remember, do not seek enlightenment. But if you must understand, practice by contemplating the mind. It is the source of all reality. The mind is the way; the inner truth. Everything arises from the mind where nothing is attained. But you should not attach yourself to your permanent mind nor should you attach yourself to your non-existent mind. To do this is to travel the middle way: this is enlightenment.

"And finally, I erase all that I have said to you with these farewell words:

"It doesn't matter how much you meditate, or study the scriptures, or give of yourself; toward patience, toward wisdom, toward discipline, toward progress, it doesn't matter your level of attainment; even austerity is an attachment. This is not dharma practice. This is being holy. But. . .if you continuously shed your layers of desire from your karma and shatter your armor of consciousness, then you have dharma practice.

"Goodbye, my friend. I hope you realize how to love."

Jansen did not disappear. He walked away as if. . .as if life was a dream.

I lay back down emersed in a total calm; no longer stuck in nothingness. If I was crazy, then I would happily go into an insane asylum, I thought.

I was suddenly happy. Now, I understood why I was going to that monastery. I was going there to clarify myself. I was not running away from anything.

I closed my eyes to this dream of a dream and did not wonder if I was awake or still asleep as I drifted off into another slumber.

Chapter 57
So they say.

They were all eating breakfast in the kitchen when I walked in the following morning. Bagels, cream cheese, coffee, and a newspaper dressed the gentle scene around the table. Frances stood up to greet me while Tommie responded to my presence with a genuine smile. French pushed out the empty chair opposite him with his foot in an offer for me to join them.

"You're back," Frances happily stated. She looked radiant, almost happy. She kissed me on the cheek. "Are you alright?"

"Sure," I said. "How about you?"

"Today, I'm smiling. That's the best that I can do."

"Any coffee left?"

"There's some in the percolator. We actually brewed a pot," she said.

I poured myself a cup and sat down with them.

"So, where's Janet?" I asked.

"She's staying with her mother," French answered.

"That's right." I'd forgotten. "I hope everything works out between you and her, French."

"Yeah, well, it's hopeless. What can I say."

I nodded my head with empathy and then looked at Frances.

"Forgive me?"

"Of course. Don't be silly. We've all made a mess of things. But. . .somehow. . .I believe we're all going to come out better in the long run. I hope, anyway." She noted my somber mood. "Hey, you did some good. I'm no longer with Drew; that means something. And maybe, just maybe, I won't try to kill myself, again." She looked at Tommie. "But I can't promise anybody that. I can't promise anything."

Tommie took her by the hand.

"But she and I are going to try to make a go of it." Tommie looked at me. "We've had all day and all night together. That alone isn't much but. . ." He looked at Frances and she finished the thought for him.

"It was an honest day and night. And I found out that we were equal. Maybe we're just equally screwed up, but we're equal. And that's a start; that. . .and one day at a time. For me, that's more important than love, right now."

An uneasy silence surfaced between us.

"Sounds like you're a lot better off without me," I said.

"Well, at least you bought me cigarettes," she smiled.

I was glad for the lightness of her remark. I smiled back.

"Well," I said. "I think it's about time I pack up and leave."

"Where are you going?" French asked.

"To a Zen monastery in California," I said.

"A what?" Tommie asked.

I pulled out the brochure from my book and placed it on the table to show them.

"This monastery. The place is called Mountain Echo Monastery."

"Where did you get this?" Frances asked.

"Out of this book that I bought from a used bookstore in The Grove."

"I see," she said without judgment as she flipped through the brochure, then handed it to Tommie.

"Anyway, it's where I want to go. It's sudden, I know, but sometimes. . .that's the way things work."

She looked at Tommie. "I know." Then she looked at me. "I hope you find yourself."

"They say that when one finds himself, one discovers that there is nothing there," I said.

"I wouldn't know anything about that," she said.

"Then that makes two of us," I said. I looked at French as I rose from my chair to go pack my bags. "I owe you money." I reached into my pocket and gave him half of what I had.

"What's this?" French asked.

"I owe you a lot more than this," I said.

"I don't need your money."

"But this is nothing," I said.

"Put it away," he insisted. "Now that you're leaving here, you're really going to need it."

I put the money back into my pocket.

"Okay," I said. "Be a good guy all the way to the end."

We chuckled. Then French offered me the affection of a handshake.

"Take care of yourself, crazyman," he said.

"You too," I said. "And thanks for everything."

"I didn't do anything."

I offered my hand to Tommie and we shook hands warmly.

"Be careful," he said.

"You too," I said.

Then I looked at Frances as she got up from her seat and came around the table to me. She kissed me on the cheek. There was no more to be said between us.

"Can I drop you off some place?" French asked.

"Yeah. I'd appreciate a ride to the bus station after I pack my bag. Can you handle that?"

"Sure. I can handle anything, remember?"

Epilogue
. . . and live.

My bus was parked in the second bay of the terminal with its engine idling. It appeared to be waiting to leave on schedule.

The bus was bound for New Orleans. That's where I was going to make my first change-over. The anonymity of the bus felt good even though the seats didn't. I sat by a dark tinted window and an elderly lady sat by the aisle next to me. We didn't speak. She was eating a bran muffin and I was studying my brochure once again: reading between the lines; imagining myself in some of the monastic settings that were represented in the photographs.

A twinge of doubt suddenly took hold of me. I was almost in a panic. I sat up with concern.

They would simply have to take me! I thought.

I relaxed back into my seat. I decided I wasn't going to worry. I shut my eyes momentarily and regained my composure.

I looked to my left and caught the elderly lady staring at me or, more likely, my black eye. She had eaten her muffin.

"I'm sorry," she said. "Are you alright?"

"I hope I didn't startle you," I said.

"Oh, no, don't mind me. I'm just nosey. Did you remember what it was you forgot?"

I'm sure my eyes must have registered confusion. I managed a smile. "No, I didn't forget anything."

"I saw my husband do what you just did, many times. He'd come home, eat dinner, then sit down to read the evening paper. Then suddenly, he'd bolt straight up in his chair as if he forgot something. He had such an intense look on his face. He'd always tell me that it was about something he'd forgotten to do at work that day. Of course, I knew that wasn't the truth. Then again, he did have a stressful job. And then again, everyone should have their own secrets. Don't you think?"

"Yes," I said as I grinned. "And what's your secret?" I teased.

"Oh, go on," she chuckled. "You want a muffin?"

"No, thank you."

"They're fresh."

"I'm sure they are.

The sound of the air brakes releasing and the bus's door closing brought our attention to the activity of the bus. When it pulled out of the station, I saw French leaning against his parked car. He couldn't see me but he knew I was on that bus. He waved, lazily. I felt compelled to wave back.

"A friend of yours?" the lady asked.

"Yes," I answered.

"Any place special?" This time she was referring to the brochure in my hand.

"Yes. I think."

"I'm sorry. I told you I was nosey."

"I think you're very nice," I said. "Everybody calls me Llewellen."

"I'm glad to meet you. My name is Ida."

"Hello, Ida."

"Friends or family in New Orleans?"

"California is where I'm going," I said.

"My, that's a long way on a bus."

"Do you still have that muffin?" I asked, to get her off the subject of my destination.

"Certainly do. I also have a thermos of coffee. You're welcome to some."

"That sounds delicious."

I folded the brochure into my pocket and shared the trip to New Orleans with this nice lady. We became traveling friends; the kind who understand that they would never see each other again.

When we arrived at our destination, her family was waiting for her at the terminal. She pointed to her grandchildren through the bus's window.

"There they are," she said. "Goodbye."

"Goodbye," I said. "And take care of yourself."

She nodded pleasantly as I helped her gather her things. We separated by her leaving the bus first.

I was not alone on my next bus. This time I traveled with Catherine's memory. . .or was it a dream?

*   *   *   *

It was late. The bus was dark and quiet. I had fallen asleep. Catherine appeared to me as if my eyes were wide open in complete consciousness. I was not startled the way I had been with Jansen the night before. She stood over me. Clearly. Completely. Flesh and blood. This was not a dream.

She wore a simple, light blue, cotton dress. Her complexion was as smooth as silk. Her straight auburn hair was radiant. Her green eyes sparkled.

She smiled at me but her eyes were filled with concern. As I looked at her, I remembered our laughter together. And I remembered the joy of eating, talking, dreaming, and loving together. I finally heard myself speak.

"Are you real?"

"I am," she answered. "But you're not. You're living a life of half-truths."

"What do you mean?" I asked in my defense.

"You think by keeping people from committing suicide that you are saving their lives, but you're not. You talk of compassion but you don't really understand it. You have to save your own life first before you can help others."

"To find myself is where my present destination leads," I said.

"I'm not so sure that where you are going is the right place for you. But I won't stop you. I love you. I want you happy again. And if I can't be here, then I must leave you in the same manner as your friend, Jansen."

"How do you know about Jansen?"

"I'm your mind, remember? I know everything about you. For your own good, erase me from your existence. Store me away in your memory and get on with your life. Go away. . .and live."

She departed from me by walking into the mist of my mind.

I was no longer sad. She was only dead; like Jansen. This realization liberated me from a pervasive darkness within me.

Yes, she was my wife. Yes, I had loved her more than anybody in this world. Yes, I would survive without her, now that I knew she was me and. . .forever in my mind. And to forget her was to be with her, forever. . .and live. . .

205

altered forever
the same forever, still
forever is a word

My mind became a blank. The extinction of slumber enveloped
me.

About D. S. Lliteras

D. S. Lliteras is an internationally published poet and a playwright with several productions to his credit. His first book, *In A Warrior's Romance*, which is a collection of haiku and photographs from the Vietnam War, was published in 1991. His first novel, *In The Heart of Things,* was published in 1992. Both works have won wide critical acclaim. *Into the Ashes* is the second novel in a trilogy, to be followed by *Half Hidden By Twilight* in 1994.

Mr. Lliteras holds a Master of Fine Arts degree in theatre from Florida State University. He is a decorated Vietnam War veteran, has been a college instructor, a theatrical director, a merchant mariner, a naval officer, a deep sea diver, and a professional firefighter.

He currently resides in Virginia Beach, Virginia, with his wife of 22 years, Dr. Kathleen Touchstone.

886271

Hampton Roads publishes a variety of books on metaphysical, spiritual, health-related, and general interest subjects. Would you like to be notified as we publish new books in your area of interest? If you would like a copy of our latest catalog, just call toll-free, (800) 766-8009, or send your name and address to:

Hampton Roads Publishing Company, Inc.
891 Norfolk Square
Norfolk, VA 23502